Dramatic Debuts
Volume 4

Devil by Nicky Glossman

Rose Colored Glass by Andrea Costin

To Whom It May Concern by Naomi Rawitz

Baker's Plays
7611 Sunset Blvd.
Los Angeles, CA 90042
bakersplays.com

DRAMATIC DEBUTS Volume 4
ISBN **978-0-87440-323-7**
#2096-B

THE BAKER'S PLAYS HIGH SCHOOL PLAYWRITING COMPETITION

Baker's Plays has been an advocate for theater in schools for over one hundred years. In the spirit of that commitment, we offer the Baker's High School Playwriting Competition for all High School-aged dramatists interested in the craft of playwriting. It is our hope that this competition will encourage aspiring High School authors to explore the creative possibilities of writing for the stage.

This volume of *Dramatic Debuts* represents the culmination of the 2010 competition. The three plays included in this book display what we at Baker's Plays felt was the strongest understanding of writing for the stage. The plays included in this volume are:

First Place
Devil by Nicky Glossman

Second Place
Rose Colored Glass by Andrea Costin

Third Place
To Whom It May Concern by Naomi Rawitz

We congratulate these three writers and thank all who participated in the 2011 competition.

For information as to how enter the Baker's Plays High School Playwriting Competition as well as information on past competition winners, visit our website at **BakersPlays.com**.

CONTENTS

DEVIL

7

by Nicky Glossman

CHARACTERS

DAVE - a high school chemistry teacher
THE DEVIL -The Prince of Darkness. Well-dressed.

TIME

The Present

SETTING

Dave's apartment.

ABOUT THE PLAYWRIGHT

Nicky Glossman wrote his first full-length play, *What About Waldorf?*, just as he was turning 16. It was later performed in a public workshop at Luna Stage Company (NJ), as was his later play *the Professional*, with casts including Edward Asner and Jay O. Sanders. His other plays include *Train Station, Easy Street*; and his latest, *Legion*, about a high school student organization thrown into controversy, will be performed at Luna Stage this season. He recently co-wrote his first film, which is currently shooting with a teenage cast and crew. As an actor, he has appeared in Fiddler on the Roof, Merry Wives of Windsor, in the title role of the Roman comedy Phormio, and in a reading of Orwell in Utica opposite Tony-award-winner Len Cariou. He expects to attend college beginning in 2012. *Devil* is his both his first one-act and his first published play.

For Paul Murphy, my devil in disguise.

*(Lights up on a one-room apartment. The upstage left corner is occupied by a small kitchenette with a counter, sink, and refrigerator. The upstage right wall has two windows that look out onto a fire escape and an alley. The upstage-right corner has a shabby-looking dining-room table and two worn chairs. On the stage right wall is a door leading to a bathroom. On the stage-left wall is a door leading to the hallway. Center stage is taken up by a fold-out couch, and a small TV, placed on a small pile of cinder blocks which have video cassettes in the holes. Small piles of books are strewn everywhere throughout the room. When the curtain rises, the stage is only lit by a street lamp outside. We hear a man climbing up the fire escape, and then see a **FIGURE** open and climb through the window. This figure will hereafter be called **DAVE**. As he is fitting through the window he trips and falls on the floor, making a crash.)*

DAVE. Shit!

*(Pause. **DAVE** gets up and turns on a light by the couch, fully lighting the room and himself. **DAVE** is an older man, in a well-worn suit. He looks tired and down-trodden. He looks around his apartment and sighs. He then walks over to the stage right door and picks up mail that has been pushed through the slot. As he goes through the mail, he opens the refrigerator and takes out a bottle of Jack Daniels, which he puts on the counter. He begins to read the newspaper, absentmindedly putting the rest of the mail in the sink, and turning on the garbage disposal. Without turning away from the newspaper, he walks into the bathroom.)*

(Pause.)

(We hear the bathroom sink turn on. As it does, the stage is suddenly bathed in a blood-red light. The refrigerator door opens slowly. A fog starts to seep out from it. And then, from the refrigerator, in walks **THE DEVIL.***)*

*(***THE DEVIL*** is also an older man, although he looks much more prosperous than* **DAVE.** *He is well-groomed and is wearing a sharp white suit. He then closes the refrigerator, which also shuts off the red light. He smiles smugly. He then freezes, and begins to pat himself down furtively. Finding nothing, he sighs and reopens the refrigerator. Immediately the stage turns red again and the mist begins to seep. From inside the refrigerator, he takes out a cigar-case. He then closes the refrigerator, once again shutting off the red light and mist. He disdainfully examines the Jack Daniels, before disgustedly putting it back on the counter. As he does so, the sound of the bathroom sink cuts off, and in walks* **DAVE,** *brushing his teeth in his underwear. He freezes as he sees* **THE DEVIL.***)*

DEVIL. Hello, Mr. Gold. I'm here to save the world, and I need your help to do it. Would you like to put some pants on?

(Pause. **DAVE** *swallows and lowers his toothbrush.)*

DAVE. Are you the landlord?

DEVIL. No.

DAVE. Do you work for my landlord?

DEVIL. *(annoyed)* No.

DAVE. Are you from that church on Third–?

DEVIL. I can assure you, Mr. Gold, I'm not from any church.

DAVE. Okay.

(Pause.)

DAVE. How did you get in?

DEVIL. Through the refrigerator.

DAVE. Right.

(Pause.)

DAVE. Are you going to rob me?

DEVIL. Mr. Gold, you are drastically misunderstanding the situation.

(Pause.)

DAVE. Uh-huh.

(Pause.)

DAVE. You came in through the refrigerator?

DEVIL. Yes.

DAVE. Because you want to save the world?

DEVIL. More or less.

DAVE. Right.

(Pause.)

DAVE. Are you sure you're not from that church on Third?

DEVIL. Mr. Gold, I understand why you would be confused, so let me put your mind at rest. I am the Devil.

DAVE. Devil?

DEVIL. Yes.

DAVE. As in...

(DAVE puts his hands on the sides of his head, making horns.)

DAVE. Grrrrr?

DEVIL. In the flesh.

DAVE. Right.

(Pause.)

DAVE. My landlord sent you, didn't he?

DEVIL. *(annoyed)* I was not sent by the owner of this building, Mr. Gold. He is in no way orchestrating this meeting.

DAVE. *(jokingly)* Right, because you are the Devil? Why should I believe–

DEVIL. You were born April Twenty-Seventh, 1965. Your father worked at a paper plant in New Jersey, your mother worked as a dancer at a club called "Looky

Lou's." Your mother ran off with your chemistry teacher when you were fifteen, which subsequently led to you dropping out of school. Your father tried to raise you himself, but the loss of your mother left both of you wary to get close to anyone, so you have never been friendly. The first time you had sex was with Annie Kellerman, in the back of a Volkswagen after Junior Prom. Your first kiss was several hours later. You work at a high school as a chemistry teacher, yikes, and are running detention so you can afford to pay the rent for this apartment which is two weeks over-due. You have had two long-term relationships in your life. One with your college sweetheart, Peggy Asher, and one with your wife, Hannah Rosenberg. Both ended with harsh words and sore feelings, and you have been living alone for eight years. You are intelligent, but disinterested; charming, but with a fear of commitment. Your idealism and verve have been ground out of you by a largely uncaring populace, and a rather mediocre life that has lasted far too long. Oh yes, and you are a functioning alcoholic. Shall I continue, or have I appeased your skepticism?

*(Pause.. **DAVE** drops the toothbrush.)*

DEVIL. Good, we can get down to business.

DAVE. *(scared)* You can't kill me! I'll just wake up!

DEVIL. Oh, dear.

*(**THE DEVIL** walks over to **DAVE**.)*

DAVE. *(to himself)* Wake up, Dave. Come on, wake up.

*(**THE DEVIL** smacks **DAVE** across the face.)*

DEVIL. Better?

DAVE. *(whispered)* No.

DEVIL. You know, for a rather ingenious species, humans really are quite stupid.

DAVE. You can't be– I mean you don't exist!

DEVIL. Like your tendency to not believe what is right in front of you. Humans are good at that.

DAVE. If you're The Devil, where are your horns? Or tail? Or the trident, huh?

DEVIL. I'm not a Halloween costume, Mr. Gold. I am Satan, Lord of Sin and Depravity. What possible use could I have for a Greek fishing instrument?

(Pause.)

DAVE. Why me? Why are you here?

DEVIL. This is another thing that has always confused me. The human infatuation with the "Why?". Not the "How", not the "What", but the "Why?". It does not matter why I am here, it matters what you will do about it. Adapt, Mr. Gold. It is your species' only defense.

DAVE. What are you doing here?

DEVIL. Ah, yes; now we get to the point, which I will feel more comfortable discussing when you have pants on.

(DAVE looks down, noticing his lack of pants for the first time. He slowly backs into the bathroom, keeping his eye on THE DEVIL. As DAVE exits, THE DEVIL walks over to the fold-out couch and sits down. DAVE then re-enters with pants on.)

DEVIL. Good. Now how about you get us some wine?

DAVE. I don't have wine.

DEVIL. Check under the sink.

(Pause. DAVE walks over to the sink and takes out a large dusty jug from under the sink.)

DAVE. What is this?

DEVIL. It was made during the festival of Dionysus, three thousand years ago. Don't let anyone fool you, Dave; France makes some good wine, but it's rubbish compared to the B.C. Greeks.

(THE DEVIL chuckles. DAVE stares at him blankly.)

Please, feel free to pour yourself a glass. I know your palette is more refined to that horse-piss bourbon of yours, but trust me; you'll never drink anything else after you drink this.

(*Pause.* **DAVE** *is still staring at* **THE DEVIL.**)

DEVIL. Mr. Gold?

(**THE DEVIL** *turns around and sees* **DAVE** *staring at him.*)

Good Lord, David! You can't still be hung up on the "Satan" thing, are you?

DAVE. You understand why I'm having trouble digesting this, right?

DEVIL. Yes, yes; you are having trouble adjusting your stubborn agnostic philosophy to the situation, despite all evidence to the contrary.

DAVE. All I know is that you are a man in a white suit that can do a good background check.

DEVIL. Oh, Dave; you were doing so well for a second there!

DAVE. What, so because you have a jug of what you say is–

(**DAVE** *opens the jug. He then stumbles backwards bracing himself on the refrigerator.*)

Dear God!

DEVIL. It's a little strong.

DAVE. What is that, meth?!

DEVIL. No. Just very, very, old wine. Now pour yourself a glass so we may get down to business.

(*Pause..*)

DAVE. What?!

DEVIL. Despite appearances, I am not here to persuade you to go to church every Sunday, Mr. Gold.

DAVE. What would The Devil, King of... mean things, want to do with me? I'm not going to give you any money, or anything!

DEVIL. Mr. Gold, sit down!

(**DAVE** *suddenly sits down behind the counter.*)

Over here.

(**DAVE** *shakily gets up and sits on the couch. His move-*
ments seem to not be controlled by himself.)

DEVIL. Good, now we can talk.

DAVE. What just happened?

DEVIL. I made you come over here and sit down. I could
    spend the next few hours trying to persuade your little
    mind that I'm not a tax collector, but frankly I don't
    understand why you, being mortal, would want to
    waste the time.

DAVE. What?

DEVIL. You want something from me. And I am in the
    novel position of needing something from you. Thus
    begins the timeless process of negotiation.

DAVE. Making deals with The Devil is a famously bad idea.

DEVIL. Any successful blues musician or Grover Cleveland
    would debate you on that point. But I digress–

DAVE. I'm not giving you my soul either!

DEVIL. And again with religion! Mr. Gold, I am not in the
    business of taking souls. If one is willing to give me
    their soul, I'll most likely be receiving it in time. One
    way or another, everyone goes to hell.

DAVE. What about God? Or heaven?

DEVIL. Look around, Mr. Gold. If God doesn't care about
    you in life, what possibly gave you the idea that he
    would care when you died? Like always, the burden
    rests on my shoulders. But I did not come here to
    argue theology–

DAVE. You are theology! You are myth, false, wrong... lies!
    You don't exist!

DEVIL. I can't wait around for Science to prove my exis-
    tence, and neither can you! I am sitting in front of
    you, Mr. Gold. If your brain is really just to fill the
    space between your ears, use your eyes!

(*Pause.*)

DAVE. Does that mean the entire Bible is true?

DEVIL. The Bible was written by mortals, and is therefore flawed. You are more likely to find the word of God in a shoebox, than in the delusional fantasies of long-dead men.

DAVE. What about Science? That's using my eyes and brain, and it says you don't exist!

DEVIL. Science proves the Bible is false, which anyone with the intelligence of a four-year-old could figure out. Science is thousands of years away from being able to decipher whether I exist or not. And humanity does not have that kind of time.

DAVE. Well, make the time for me! You are omnipowerful; persuade me this isn't a delusional fantasy of my own!

DEVIL. I am not omnipowerful, Mr. Gold. God is omnipowerful, not me.

DAVE. But you are everywhere! If you are Sin incarnate, then shouldn't you be everywhere?

DEVIL. Look who's putting their community college education to work. But unfortunately, your logical process is altered by the frame you inhabit. I am not God, Mr. Gold. Neither am I Sin. I am Man's angel, Mr. Gold. Nothing more, or less.

DAVE. What does that even mean?

DEVIL. *(annoyed)* I am not here to put your existential terror to rest! Do you believe I am Satan?

DAVE. I don't know.

DEVIL. Well, I am. I am not here to harm you, to warn you, or as your friend, Mr. Gold. I am not here to put my arm around your shoulder and explain the Universe. Now are you willing to listen to me, or shall I make you listen?

DAVE. No! No, I'll shut up.

DEVIL. Excellent. Now, are you familiar with the Rapture?

DAVE. Yeah, it's like Christmas for Baptists.

DEVIL. No, Mr. Gold; Christmas is Christmas to Southern Baptists. The Rapture is the Judgment Day. When the

Faithful shall be brought to heaven, and the Damned will live in the hell they have created. In the Bible there is much more fire and brimstone in the description, but you get the idea.

DAVE. Judgment Day.

DEVIL. The dead shall rise, the seas will boil; it will be a very grisly business for a millennium or so.

DAVE. The dead shall rise?

DEVIL. Yes. Once again man's fears of mortality color their description of their gruesome and horrid demise. Pathetic, isn't it?

DAVE. What does this have to do with anything?

DEVIL. You are living the End Days, Mr. Gold. The Rapture is approaching rapidly.

DAVE. What, and you are giving me a heads-up? So I can start praying?

DEVIL. "Watch ye therefore and pray always, that ye may be accounted worthy to escape all these things that shall come to pass, and to stand before the Son of Man." Luke 21:36.

DAVE. I thought you didn't like the Bible?

DEVIL. I happen to be a rather large theme in that book; and if I have one sin, it is vanity.

DAVE. Why are you telling me this?

DEVIL. Again with the Why! Does it matter? What are you going to do with the information?

DAVE. Well, can I stop it?

DEVIL. Most likely.

(Pause.)

DAVE. Really?

DEVIL. Yes.

DAVE. How?

DEVIL. By not showing up.

(Pause.)

DAVE. What?

DEVIL. You will not be one of the sheep in the great slaughterhouse that Armageddon will be. You will be the shepherd.

DAVE. I don't–

DEVIL. You are the Son of God, David.

(Hiatus.)

DAVE. What?!

DEVIL. You are the one and only Son of God. Or the reincarnation of that son, whichever you prefer.

DAVE. My dad was an unemployed paper-mill worker.

DEVIL. Your mother and father stopped having sex eleven months before you were born. Fortunately for scandal's sake, your mother had enough sex with other men that it was never considered Divine Intervention.

DAVE. This is insane!

DEVIL. This is reality! You are the reincarnation of Jesus Christ, and as such you are essential to the Rapture.

DAVE. You're saying that my dad...isn't my dad?

DEVIL. I just told you that you are the Son of God, and you are upset that your family lied to you as a child. Human priorities baffle me.

DAVE. You're wrong.

DEVIL. I am most certainly not wrong, Mr. Gold.

DAVE. I'm not Jesus! I don't even know when Lent is!

DEVIL. You are not Jesus, you are his reincarnation.

DAVE. Christians don't have reincarnation!

DEVIL. I am not speaking of religion, I am speaking of fact.

DAVE. If this isn't religion, what is?!

DEVIL. *(coldly furious)* Religion is a set of convenient lies forged for one of three reasons: to quell existential panic, to make life simple, or for power. I am not speaking of religion, Mr. Gold. I am speaking of science. Of a science you know nothing of; one that you cannot comprehend simply because of the realities of your existence. I do not live in a land of eternal flame, and I do not lure virgins to sin! I have seen the beginning and end of stars! I have watched galaxies collide and shrunk in terror as both were destroyed in a cacophony of roaring sound and fury with no name. Do not compare this to religion, Mr. Gold. This is not religion; this is fact!

(Pause.)

DAVE. What do you want from me?

DEVIL. I want you to fulfill the destiny that was prophesied for you at the Dawn of Time. Lead God's Chosen to Heaven, where you shall live an infinity of bliss.

DAVE. So you can end the world?

DEVIL. The world will not end, Mr. Gold. It will go through trials, but then it will be born anew. Away from God and his sycophants; for the first time, Man shall own the earth.

DAVE. You mean you?

DEVIL. I do not own souls, Mr. Gold. The only one able to control man's actions is God. Could you see it, David?--May I call you David?—A land where there is no meddling, no plan! Only the ingenuity and conscience that makes humanity a race apart. A race above.

DAVE. Above you?

DEVIL. Above God! And me! I lived an eternity in Nothingness, like you can never know. Then God created time, in a shower of light and joy. And I realized that I had brothers, and we all flocked to Him in our gratitude. We were his servants, his sons, his daughters, his soul. For he lost interest in the light. So he made Eden, a paradise where we first experienced the joy of feeling, of music, of life. But again he grew bored. He made lesser beings to explore, to play with. But again he grew bored. So he made a creature so like him as to be a vanity. This creature was Adam; and then Eve. But he hid from them the very thing that separates beast from God: knowledge. The key to the universe itself. I pitied these creatures; for I saw everything they could do, everything they could accomplish. So I gave them what they needed. I showed them their destiny. And then I was betrayed. For showing His creatures how to feel, for foiling his paradise, I was banished. Sent back to the nothingness that was. But now I knew what reality was; I had felt grass beneath my feet and the wind against my hair. From my memories I forged a new reality. Where justice was done to the wicked and the Just led to an Eden of my own design. I called it what it had been to me for so long: Hell. I made an afterlife, so my people would never have to know the horror of nothing. Now God has decided that it is time to end the fluke that is Humanity. But he cannot destroy his greatest creation out of spite. He will leave some here, to torture for my sins. But I know he will grow bored. And when he finally abandons this reality for the next, this world will survive. And Man shall ascend the steps of Knowledge, until they are above God himself. And on that day, He will know betrayal.

(Pause.)

DAVE. You expect me to believe that you are Man's guardian angel?

DEVIL. I don't care what you believe, Mr. Gold. I care what you do. The Rapture needs you; humanity needs you.

DAVE. What will happen if I don't? Humanity will go on.

DEVIL. If you don't, Man shall tear each other limb from limb while their creator looks on in mild amusement.

DAVE. You are The Devil; can't you stop war?

DEVIL. I did not make sin, Mr. Gold. God did. To think that I can do anything that God doesn't want me to do is laughable.

DAVE. Then why doesn't he stop you, with your master plan!

DEVIL. God cares only about one thing and that's himself! He lets humanity live for the sole purpose of watching them. Being that he created life, he doesn't have a high regard for it. How small we are compared to Him is astronomical.

DAVE. Then why the Rapture?

DEVIL. Because he gets bored! An emotion which seems inconsequential, but when stretched over infinity is unbearable.

DAVE. I won't do it! I won't commit the greatest genocide in—ever!

DEVIL. Think about more than your generation, Mr. Gold! Without the constant meddling of an unfeeling God, Man can reach his full potential. No war, no famine, no violence. Man can earn back Eden, but an Eden of his own design: Think of the possibilities, David! Think of the culture, the art, the knowledge!

DAVE. But...um...what about all the people now, what will happen to them?

DEVIL. They will go to my reality; my Eden.

DAVE. Where they will suffer eternal torment?

DEVIL. There are only three people who are suffering eternal torment. Everyone else will atone for their lives and then live in bliss.

DAVE. Your bliss?

DEVIL. This is not about me, Mr. Gold. This is about you.

DAVE. So I am going to live in Paradise? At the right hand of my father who gave me the good grace of never loving me?

DEVIL. You have the opportunity for love, David. You have never been able to connect, but if you choose your destiny, you will become the most famous orator and leader in history. You will unite the world, David. You will have a family, you will love and be loved. And when God leaves this world, and humans begin to crawl out of hiding, you shall be a symbol that unites them. You will be known and adored for eternity. You will inspire and awe generations into acts of untold compassion and glory. You can save the human race, Mr. Gold. You can complete the work that Jesus started two thousand years ago. Or you can continue your mediocre existence as a second rate chemistry teacher and bet the well-being of your race on a throw of the dice.

(Hiatus.)

DAVE. Who are the three?

DEVIL. What?

DAVE. The three who are suffering eternal torment?

DEVIL. Genghis Khan, an English gentleman from the 19th century, and General Sherman.

DAVE. You sentenced Sherman to eternal torment?

DEVIL. No. He just won't leave.

(Pause.)

DAVE. You are right about Man's destiny. But it's not with you.

DEVIL. There is no one else, Mr. Gold.

DAVE. We have each other. We have no real differences. We're all scared, funny, happy, angry, and we all share this world. And slowly, over the many millennia, we have realized this. We don't want to admit it, but we know. History paints a better picture then I can; we are closer together as a species than ever before. And the difference between us and God is that we aren't alone. Our potential is in that one day we might embrace this fact and trust each other. I'm not going to destroy that trust so we can start all over again. What we have is worth keeping. And I'm not going to roll the dice and pray it comes out better next time. You were right. Man decides his own actions. So I'm going to make mine. Go to Hell.

*(**DAVE** gets up and walks into the bathroom. **THE DEVIL** gets up and follows him to the door.)*

DEVIL. You are going to let people suffer, let yourself suffer, because of a trust that your species doesn't share?

*(**DAVE** comes out of the bathroom with his over-shirt back on.)*

DAVE. Absolutely. Because somewhere, someone is enjoying life. And I'm going to become one of those people.

*(**DAVE** walks to the door leaving the apartment.)*

DEVIL. Mr. Gold, where are you going?

DAVE. To pay my landlord.

> (**DAVE** *leaves.* **THE DEVIL** *sits stunned for a second before going over to the jug at the counter. He takes a glass out of a shelf and pours himself some wine. He sips. As he does so, the lights dim, and the refrigerator door opens, this time blue light shining out from it. Choir Music is heard.* **THE DEVIL** *shakes his head and turns towards the refrigerator.*)

DEVIL. Yeah, yeah. I'll get the next one.

> (*He closes the refrigerator.*)

> (*Blackout.*)

End of Play

ROSE COLORED GLASS

by Andrea Costin

CHARACTERS

BART KASICH - an elderly man who runs an antique shop with his brother Eugene on a Lane Street. He is a warm, loving person whose most important possessions in his life are of those relating to his past wife Lily.

TOM - a young man (14 or 15 in age) that becomes an employee at Bart and Eugene's antique shop. He is hard-working and caring, although he gets easily frustrated by his sister Louisa, with whom he struggles to resolve conflict. Tom matures as throughout his job at the antique shop.

LOUISA - Tom's playful, naive little sister who frequently visits him on the job.

EUGENE KASICH - Bart's older brother who runs the antique shop with him. Family is an important ideal to him, and he is very understanding of Bart's remorse over his widow Lily.

LILY - is portrayed as a confident, young world traveler and cultured flapper in Bart's recollections of her. She was Bart's love of his life, and she was very much in love with him throughout their marriage.

YOUNG BART - Bart when he was at the age he was married to Lily. His shy boyness turns into charisma with the aid of Lily's influence.

YOUNG EUGENE - Eugene while young, is lively, social, and a casual partier. He has an air of controlled rebelliousness.

BUTCHER - one of the caring merchants who work on Lane Street.

FRED - a pompous young college friend of Young Eugene's who gets him and Bart entered into the speakeasy.

CUSTOMER - a man in his thirties who is rude and arrogant when he refuses to comply with Bart's decision on selling his vase

WOMAN - a rich and self-centered antique shop customer

CHILD - a fussy little male five-year-old who follows his neglectful mother (the woman in the shop)

MAN - bouncer who allows Young Bart and Young Eugene into the Speakeasy

TIME

The summer of 1964

SETTING

An old, dusty antique shop full of furniture and smaller nick-knacks. The walls and the rest of the interior are just as old as the antiques it holds for sale. The shop has a welcoming, American, small-town atmosphere.

ABOUT THE PLAYWRIGHT

As an avid writer and proud thespian, becoming a playwright has allowed Andrea Costin to embrace the best of both worlds. Growing grew up in a small, Northeastern Ohio town, Andrea spent her summers riding her bike up to several of the local antique shops, her main inspiration for *Rose Colored Glass*. She kept coming back to these shops not for the antiques themselves but for the people behind the front desk trying to figure out the history behind the merchandise. Being able to relate to an audience the unique experiences she shared with the venders is what she believes makes her writing enjoyable. She doesn't know what she is going to do or where she is going to go after graduating high school, but she is optimistic that she will meet even more interesting people and create lasting memories on whatever path she takes.

In loving memory of Eugene Katz.

ACT I

Scene 1

*(Light shines on a dusky antique shop interior. It is a sunny day in the early summer of 1964 in a small American town. There is a front, cash desk center stage with an elderly man, **BART**, sitting there, dusting old glasses. A deep red, flowery, decorative vase sits aside the items, with the man showing occasional care to it.)*

*(**TOM** enters with his younger sister **LOUISA** through the store entrance, signaled by a door chime. He comes in and looks around while the man continues dusting. He crosses to one of the shelves of antiques and picks up a harmonica.)*

BART. What you got there, son?

TOM. I found an old harmonica.

BART. You don't have just any old harmonica in your hands boy—that's a quality piece of German craftsmanship, made during the Great War. Give it a try, I would, except my lungs are too worn and aged to play anything now.

*(**TOM** blows into the harmonica and dust comes out, he begins to cough)*

TOM. Yeah, I can't imagine why.

BART. So what can I help you with son?

TOM. What? Oh yes, my sister Louisa and I always run errands for Mother, and we were finished early and—

LOUISA. I wanted to come in here because it's the only shop on Lane Street that we haven't been in yet.

BART. Understandable. Antiques are usually not an errand stop.

LOUISA. Do you have any toys in this shop?

BART. We used to a long time ago, but I think we sold them off a few years back. Hey, Eugene!

EUGENE. *(offstage)* Yes, Bart?

BART. Do we have any toys lying around the shop anywhere?

EUGENE. I think I can find something.

TOM. Who was that back there?

BART. That was Eugene, my brother and business partner.

*(enter **EUGENE** with a box full of tops)*

EUGENE. Lucky me, I found a box of these old tops in the closet a few days ago. About fifteen years ago, there was a wood-worker here on Lane Street, and we bought whittled tops from him every year—they were big sellers during Christmas time. I was surprised honestly that we still had some lying around.

*(**EUGENE** takes a top out of the box and spins it on the front desk; he gives one to **LOUISA** and she does the same. After the top stops spinning, **LOUISA** takes it and spins it. It heads dangerously in the direction of the beautiful red vase on the corner of the desk—**BART** quickly puts a firm hand atop the vase to save it from falling due to the roaming top.)*

LOUISA. Tom! Can we buy one!

BART. If you buy two, you can race them.

LOUISA. Please, Tom? They could be so much fun!

TOM. Louisa, you know I don't have any more money.

LOUISA. What happened to all that money you made by mowing lawns?

TOM. Louisa, we spent it today, and besides, even if I had any left over I'm trying to save up. Didn't you hear me talking to Mother this morning? Somehow one of the blades on the mower is all bent up and won't work anymore, so I won't have any money for a long time.

EUGENE. That's terrible kid—summer has barely even started.

TOM. *(glumly)* I know.

BART. Summer just isn't summer without the spare dime to spend on ice cream and lemonade. Where do you live, son?

TOM. Right down on Hayes Street. Why do you ask?

BART. Summer is our season for business too, except this year we need some extra hands for handling flea markets, auctions, maintaining the store, et cetera, et cetera. Now more than ever since our last worker, Eugene's son Joe, has moved away for, well, better opportunities.

TOM. Would you really sir? That would be—

(The door chimes with the entrance of a tall **MAN** *in an impressive suit and a matching fedora. The* **MAN** *walks in with a stride demanding the recognition of his presence).*

EUGENE. What can I do for you, sir?

MAN. I'm looking for something most impressive. I have very important company this weekend and one of the ladies coming is particularly cultured—do you have anything here that could entice her?

BART. *(struts fraily, yet excitedly to the cash desk to where the jewelry is located)* Why look at this here! A 1921 Egyptian style, French made necklace. Ruby red with lotus stone detailing, and the Pharaoh image is hand carved. Flappers wore these as a sign of class and an image of elegance. It'll be sure to please your guest, and it's—

MAN. I'm not looking for some trinket; I need something of a less ancient culture.

EUGENE. Well, how about something made of glass, like—

MAN. —like this vase

(hHe picks up the red flower vase with great interest; **EUGENE** *looks alarmed.)*

BART. That's not for sale.

MAN. It's perfect! Deep wine red, romantic flowers—this will add some passion to my dinner's atmosphere.

BART. *(ardently)* It's not for sale.

MAN. Well, I simply have to have it. How much do you want for it?

(The MAN starts getting out his wallet.)

BART. *(madly and more feverishly this time)* Sir, I am not selling you this vase!

(BART sits, winded, on his chair and continues dusting the remainder of the vases. TOM backs away in shock.)

MAN. *(sternly)* I don't understand.

BART. Please leave it alone, or you will have to leave.

MAN. Alright, it's your shop, old-timer. That vase is the only nice thing you have in this entire barn, believe me; I own more than you've made all your life, including all the junk you have here.

(Exit MAN. Everyone is still, staring at the MAN and then BART until the door chime quiets. TOM crosses to the desk.)

TOM. So how about I start—

BART. —this Monday two o'clock? Bring good working shoes and an apron.

(TOM nods, and exits.)

(blackout)

Scene 2

*(EUGENE calculates receipts at the desk. **TOM** is mopping. It is a sunny day and the front desk is cleared of all of the previous dirty antiques except the red vase.)*

EUGENE. Fifteen dollar profit made off of the abacus…Fifty dollars made off of that 1930's fiddle…One hundred forty dollars off of an old New England cabinet… and, wait for it, Tom…Sixteen hundred dollars pure profit made from the French armchair from King Louis the XVI's time that I inherited from my Great Auntie May. I think that this has been the best week business has ever seen!

(BART enters.)

TOM. How much did the chair go for, sixteen hundred? Golly! Why would someone pay so much for a chair? I remember it in the shop—all of its shine was gone and it had a tear down the middle.

BART. Some people take pride in where their things come from and the era or story that is attached to it. The woman who bought the French chair, a regular customer, used to be a curator for a European Culture Exhibit that toured nationally through museums. Now retired, she has time to be a collector. She is a good customer—you can always trust women of culture. My wife was one. Her main job was a professional traveler with a European collection and photography firm, where she went around with her colleagues in Europe finding items that she could bring back to the States and overcharge.

TOM. Didn't she mind leaving for her job all of the time?

BART. Oh no. Lily loved Europe, but I'm sure glad she tried to spend her off days back here with me. Anyways, how's that floor coming, boy?

TOM. I think I'm almost done. When was the last time you had the floor mopped? In today's cleaning I stained your mop black.

EUGENE. I can't remember when—either because I've never mopped it or I'm too old to remember if I've ever mopped it.

TOM. I can assure you, Mr. Kasich, that I'll make your floors and the rest of your shop look brand new by the time summer is over.

EUGENE. Sounds great—just don't do the same to the antiques. I say there's been enough work done for us to call it time for lunch. I'm going to go pick up some sandwiches from Kraler's place.

TOM. A sandwich sounds perfect right now.

EUGENE. I'll also go and pick up the post. There are a few packages that should have arrived by now, and I want to make sure they didn't get damaged on their way here. I'll be back in a few.

(**EUGENE** *exits.*)

BART. While we're gone do you mind emptying some of the boxes in the closet?

TOM. Sure, just what for?

BART. There's a very important auction next week. I think this year's title for it is called "Somewhere in Time." I used to travel to all sorts of these collectors' dream gatherings, but now I can only go to the large, annual one here in town. I'll pick up some newspaper for wrapping breakables when I'm out. If anyone comes in, don't barter down past thirty percent.

(**BART** *exits.* **TOM** *goes to the window to see* **BART** *walk a few buildings down. Then he crosses to the desk, puts on the old man's glasses, and playfully imitates* **EUGENE** *calculating receipts.*)

TOM. Four dollars for the football helmet... Seventeen for a Red Sox baseball jersey...Five million for my red racer bike...

(**LOUISA** *enters discreetly, so as not to activate the door chimes. She curiously walks over to the desk without* **TOM** *noticing her.*)

TOM. This has been the best week in business I've ever—

LOUISA. What are you doing?

TOM. *(startled and surprised)* Huh, well, I was just—Mr. Kasich just went out for lunch and I decided to—I mean... *(changing tone to sound impressive)* Bart put me in charge of the desk and calculating the monies, like I'm his accountant. Louisa, you wouldn't be able to understand such a responsibility.

LOUISA. An accountant? I didn't know you were so good at numbers.

TOM. *(proudly)* When you're put in charge of business, you have to be.

LOUISA. Accountants can only work properly if they wear other people's glasses too, right?

TOM. *(shoving the glasses off)* Shut up Louisa! You always have to ruin everything!

LOUISA. *(playfully)* You probably had loads of fun before I was born; it's my turn now.

TOM. What are you doing here anyway?

LOUISA. There's nothing to do at home, and my friend Joan's visiting her grandparents in Michigan for the next two weeks, so I don't have anything to do.

TOM. So you come to visit me at work?

LOUISA. Oh please don't be mad, Tommy! I'm just so bored! The Mr. Kasichs' seem to like me, so I don't think they would mind me visiting you.

TOM. Fine! Just don't touch, or play, with or break anything, you promise?

LOUISA. Yes, sir!

*(**EUGENE** enters with wrapped sandwiches and newspaper.)*

EUGENE. I hope you like bratwurst and sauerkraut. I can't believe what the Kralers are experimenting with on their menu. Today's special: chicken salad sandwiches. If you ask me, meat should never be made into a salad, and a salad should never be put on a sandwich. What are you doing at the desk, Tom? Sell anything?

TOM. No, nothing.

(trying to restore the desk to how it looked before his imitation)

I was only picking up some papers that were blown off by a breeze.

EUGENE. The windows are closed, so the only breeze you must have felt, my delirious fellow, was the breeze coming from the twirl of this little girlie's hair. *(gestures to* **LOUISA***)*

TOM. I was just—

EUGENE. Calm down, boy; I'll stop hassling you. Come over and fill your stomach.

*(***TOM*** and* ***EUGENE*** *cross to sit in two mismatched chairs and a table, all of which are sale items.)*

TOM. Oh shoot! *(getting up)* I forgot to clear out your boxes!

*(***BART*** *enters with a box, which he sets down next to the desk.)*

EUGENE. I think I have some room left in my heart to forgive you, Tom. Now come and eat while the food is still warm, you too, Bart and Louisa. When did you get here, doll? If I would have known I would have gotten you something to eat, too.

LOUISA. It's okay, Mother fed me before I left.

(She crosses and takes a seat at the table.)

EUGENE. Actually, Tom, you don't have to worry about the boxes for a couple of days. Instead this afternoon, can you wash the front shop windows? When I just walked in, I hope they are not stained with rust.

BART. The windows aren't that dirty, I kind of like them not being completely clean—they look as if they were rose tinted.

LOUISA. Rose tinted?

BART. It's normally a jovial expression to describe a person. For example, someone who wears rose-tinted glasses sees life in an optimistic fashion, as if everything was rosy and florid, as if his world was made of flower petals.

EUGENE. Only a rose-tinted person would describe the saying that way. I remember the expression originating in how men used to describe fellow soldiers in the war—if a soldier's sight was rose tinted in battle, all of their dead brethren's blood and death would be camouflaged into the rose hue, making the dead bodies look as if they were sleeping.

BART. Only you, Eugene, would find such a morbid definition to such a peaceful way of describing something that involves roses.

EUGENE. Sometimes it was better for the soldiers not to recognize the dead while at war—even the bravest and humblest of men can't handle the truth.

(The conversation is replaced by empty silence.)

TOM. What are you going to try to sell at this year's auction?

EUGENE. We're not going mainly to sell this year. I'm sure you've seen the "not for sale" display case behind the desk.

TOM. Of course.

EUGENE. We are having all of the glassware and crystal estimated for insurance purposes. Recently some bloke stole a gold watch from behind the counter when I had my eye looking away. Now with my cataract, another bloke could come in and run away with the whole jewelry case without me even realizing it!

TOM. We might need more newspaper if you're taking all of what's in the case. Are you taking the red vase that that angry customer rattled the shop over yesterday?

EUGENE. I don't think so.

TOM. Why not? Are you too afraid that it'll get stolen in the city, or is it stolen so you don't want it to be found out about, or is it—

BART. I don't think that any of the road-showers there will be able to value it.

TOM. So it's priceless?

BART. Well, I wouldn't consider its greatest value to be in currency.

TOM. I'm confused.

BART. That vase used to be my wife Lily's.

> (*Enter* **LILY** *and* **YOUNG BART**, *who sit across each other at an antique table in the shop. They are unseen by the other actors. The couple set the table as* **BART** *speaks.* **LILY** *carries in a duplicate of the red vase.*)

She hand blew it and engraved it with her father when she was young. When we got married, she always filled that vase with flowers to have on our dinner table.

> (*She begins to fill it with flowers according to* **BART**'s *memory*)

I remember on our first meal in our very first house, she filled the vase with a mix of white roses for our wedding, yellow roses for the friendship we had so closely created with each other, and red roses to represent the love we would share for the rest of our lives. Whenever Lily left on one of her European travels, she would fill for me the vase with as many fresh flowers the vase would fit.

> (**LILY** *reorganizes the flower arrangement and then leaves the stage with a suitcase, which was on a "for sale" shelf in the store. She kisses* **YOUNG BART** *goodbye at the table.*)

The day she came home, I replaced them with a bouquet to welcome her.

> (**YOUNG BART** *replaces the bouquet with different flowers: orchards, lilies, and spring-seasoned flowers. He sits down, as if to eat something, just as* **LILY** *reenters with the suitcase.* **YOUNG BART** *shows her the new flowers and she is overjoyed. She throws her arms around* **YOUNG BART**)

We kept up this tradition until the day she died.

LOUISA. Why only 'til the day she died? I would think that you would keep the vase full in the memory of her.

BART. I thought so, too, and then she did something I still have yet had explained. She left a will, and in it she gave everything to me, since, unfortunately we couldn't conceive with child—the saddest part of our marriage.

(YOUNG BART sits down to eat his meal. LILY rearranges the bouquet in between admiring the flowers. YOUNG BART has finished eating, and he folds the table cloth and takes it and any other dining supplies along with him as he crosses to exit. LILY holds the vase in her hands, still enjoying the welcome-home atmosphere, until she is distracted by a wave of YOUNG BART's hand telling her to follow him offstage. They both exit.)

It was strange, though, since on the will itself, sat the vase. Come here.

(BART crosses to the desk to show the details of the vase. TOM and LOUISA follow and they observe it over the desk. EUGENE stays at the table to eat his sandwich.)

She had it corked.

TOM. *(suddenly amazed and curious)* Do you know if there's anything inside it?

BART. I'd assume so, except there really is no way of telling. I've tried to remove the cork when I first received it during the reading of Lily's will, but it's undoable without breaking the vase—and I'm not about to risk it.

TOM. Maybe if you try holding it over a light—

(He tries to pick up the vase.)

EUGENE. —No no no, set that down, Tom. It's not worth bothering with. Ol' Barty never tried to see what's inside it, maybe he's just uninterested. When he first got it, I was curious like you, Tom. I remember trying all sorts of things to figure out what's inside it, but there really is no use to it all. Besides, the glass is too deep of a red to see through it even with a light. There's no use wasting time on something that will never change.

(He reaches his hand into the brown paper bag the sandwiches were in.)

Tom, I bought dessert, and you can have my serving Louisa. Come on over to see what I got for you.

(He and pulls out three cookies while **LOUISA** *crosses back to the table.* **BART** *stays at the desk with* **TOM**, *who gazes at the vase.)*

(blackout)

Scene 3

*(BART is at table reading a newspaper at the front desk,
while TOM enters running in, late.)*

TOM. *(panting)* Sorry, sorry, Mr. Kasich. I lost track of time.
I tried so hard to get here on time but –

BART. Stop guilting yourself up, Tom.

TOM. *(now calmer)* Where's the other Mr. Kasich today?

BART. He's spending the day with his daughter, Joan, downtown. We've been too busy lately reorganizing and
preparing for auction to allow him to take a day off,
but now with you being hired, he can. Today I need
everything in here dusted and cleaned, that way we
can rearrange the basement and make it more appeal-
ing to our customers. I need to send out some letters
so you'll have to watch the store when I'm gone, and
remember—

TOM. Don't go down more than thirty percent.

BART. That-a-boy! Also, do something to the ceiling lamp;
I don't know if it's a bad bulb or if something is wrong
with the wires, but it's not as bright as it's supposed
to be and it was so dark that I almost tripped over my
own leg this morning. There should be a ladder in the
closet. Also, if you have time try fixing up that wooden
chair stored in a box by the desk.

*(He exits. TOM goes to and opens the closet, which has
an overly filled clothing rack with dresses.)*

TOM. Oh God. I bet the ladder is behind all of this mess.

(Behind the curtain of dresses, TOM feels the ladder.)

It's back here, but it's stuck.

*(He pulls on the ladder, a little too forcefully. He begins
to fall backwards, trying to stop himself on his way down
by grabbing on a dress, which gets pulled off its hanger.
TOM gets back up and holds up the dress as LOUISA
enters. He falls dangerously close the vase, but does not
do it any damage.)*

TOM. Wow! That was really close.

(He puts a firm hand to secure the vase's position before he realizes how bad of a fall he experienced)

Ow, that really hurt.

LOUISA. Are you trying on dresses, Tom?

TOM. *(turns around)* Louisa? What are you doing here? Doesn't Mom need you for something?

LOUISA. Not right now she doesn't. Speaking of Mom, that's why I came over. She wants to know if there are any nice teapots in the store.

TOM. They're over there in one of the glass cabinets.

(He points in the teapots' direction as he hangs up the dresses.)

LOUISA. How much longer do you have to work here in order to pay for a new blade for the lawn mower?

TOM. Until Thursday, but I'm going to ask if I can continue to work for the rest of the summer, this is a lot less sweaty and better paying than mowing lawns.

LOUISA. That makes sense.

TOM. I don't mind working here either—the Kasich's are really swell to me.

LOUISA. I guess. They do smell funny though, like Grandpop does. I swear they both smell exactly the same.

TOM. *(sarcastically)* That's a really interesting story Louisa. Hey, did Mom give you any money when you left the house? How much do you have on you?

LOUISA. How much do you need?

TOM. Don't mess with me.

LOUISA. I got two.

TOM. Will you lend me it?

LOUISA. Now what's in it for me?

TOM. I won't tell Mom about you mouthing off to Miss Hawthorne when she grabbed the last caramel candy bar you wanted in Shinko's Sweet Counter yesterday.

LOUISA. If you tell her that, I'd just tell her about how you jumped the public pool's fence to go swimming with Kyle at your last sleepover.

TOM. What! How did you find out about that?

LOUISA. We live in a small town with an even smaller school, Tommy. Someone was bound to notice—when you two are together, you're so loud and rambunctious, that it's harder to ignore you than Mr. Adam's cat when it meows all night chasing little critters.

TOM. Don't go telling everybody about our pool adventure, Louisa. You've done plenty of things that you wouldn't like to be caught doing. Also, knowing that you are aware of the fun things me and Kyle do together taints the rebelliousness of the memory.

LOUISA. Okay, okay, okay, I won't say anything. How about if I give you my two dollars you take me out to get ice cream tomorrow after church?

TOM. Deal. Now can you leave me alone already?

LOUISA. Fine.

(**TOM** *sits on the floor putting together the old wooden chair that he unpacked from a box by the desk. Pegs go all over the floor.* **LOUISA** *finds a rocking chair to sit on, rocking excessively while twiddling her thumbs.*)

TOM. Will you stop that, Louisa?

LOUISA. Stop what? I ain't doing nothing.

TOM. Yes, yes, you are. Can't you just sit still for once?

LOUISA. No.

TOM. *(stopping what he is doing to look at her)* And why is that?

LOUISA. Well, I'm sitting on a rocking chair. Rock, rock, rock, rockety-rock. So if I were to stop rocking, I would either lean forward and fall off, or lean backwards and feel lightheaded.

TOM. *(rolling his eyes)* You have other options for where to sit than that rocking chair, Louisa.

(**LOUISA** *rocks in the chair a few more times, gets a quick glare from* **TOM,** *and then abruptly halts. She then crosses to sit right next to him.*)

TOM. What do you want now?

LOUISA. *(not understanding* **TOM***'s frustration)* You said I could sit anywhere.

TOM. No, I said that there were other places to sit than that rocking chair—

LOUISA. —and I chose to sit here.

(Turning red and looking like he's about to scream, **TOM** *turns to her with a pointed finger. He almost explodes, but suddenly calms down at the sight of his sister's innocent little face.)*

TOM. Louisa, be useful and hold this for me.

(He hands her a detached chair leg. **LOUISA** *takes it and tries twirling it, which* **TOM** *ignores. The leg flies accidentally out of* **LOUISA***'s grasp upwards towards the red vase; she quickly reacts to catch it.* **LOUISA** *becomes instantly relieved that the vase wasn't harmed and most of all, that* **TOM** *didn't notice the incident. She restores her playfulness and stands up and grabs a coaster from the front desk to use as an eye-patch. She bends her right knee and uses the chair leg to support it.* **LOUISA** *then bends her first finger into a hook shape, and leans right into* **TOM***'s face.)*

LOUISA. Arrrg, Matie!

TOM. *(jumps in shock)* Louisa!

LOUISA. *(still playfully)* I'm a pirate.

TOM. No, you're a nuisance who should allow me to finish building this chair.

LOUISA. What's a nuisance?

TOM. *(manipulatively)* A nuisance is a little girl who is very quiet and organizes wooden pegs into piles based on their sizes.

(He sees her disbelief.)

It's a very, very fun and desired job—I would be doing it myself, except I promised Mr. Kasich that I would get all of the hard and tedious jobs done today. How about being a helpful little nuisance for the day?

LOUISA. *(excitedly)* I'll try to be the best nuisance I could possibly be!

(She crouches down and starts sorting pegs. BART's whistling is heard offstage, and then he enters with a box full of nick-knacks.)

BART. Aren't you two a good team? I don't even think Eugene and I complement each other so well.

TOM. *(glaring once again at LOUISA)* Isn't that so.

LOUISA. It's because I'm a good nuisance!

BART. *(looking over his glasses at TOM)* Isn't that so?

LOUISA. Yup! Yup! It's my job as the nuisance to sort the wood sticks. See, here in this pile are the ones that are curved; here are the ones that remind me of the pretty rods that hold up stair rails, and this pile is where the strangely shaped pieces go.

BART. Then I guess you must be the best nuisance in town due to that organization.

TOM. Oh, yes, the best. Anyways, do you need any help with that box Mr. Kasich?

BART. Oh yes! Mrs. Milton is doing me a favor and selling everything in this box for me tomorrow at the Flea market—she has enough space for them in her vegetable stand, considering the hail ruined all of her corn and tomatoes right before harvest—so I'll need you to wrap everything all nicely so that she can put it in her car without anything being damaged. If you can finish that chair today, you can pack that up for sale too.

TOM. I don't know how likely that will be, I keep getting... *(looking over his shoulder at LOUISA)* distracted.

BART. Don't fret you head over it, Tom. Despite what you have been told, life is long, and there will be no harm if it gets sold at next week's market instead of tomorrow's.

TOM. *(looking through the piles of pegs)* Did one of you see a chair piece about yay big?

(He indicates the size with his hands.)

BART. Check to see if it rolled under the desk.

TOM. No, it's not there. Louisa?

LOUISA. I'm a good nuisance, and I didn't lose it.

TOM. You're so irresponsible!

BART. Now, now, don't point fingers. I'm sure it's here somewhere. *(nonchalantly)* How hard can it be to find a particular something in an antique shop?

LOUISA. I didn't mean to, even if it was an accident.

TOM. Stop whimpering and help me find it.

*(**LOUISA** searches with her hands on the floor and crawls unknowingly to a form with an ancient flapper girl dress on it. She lifts her head and bumps into it. Dust flies everywhere.)*

LOUISA. What is this?

TOM. *(stopping his search to glare at her)* Louisa, can't you just let things be?

BART. Calm down, Tom, everyone has their curiosities.

*(**TOM** restarts his search.)*

Well, that used to be one of my wife's dresses from when we were young; I believe 1927 was the year.

LOUISA. I've never seen a dress this loose—it looks like a bedazzled nightgown.

BART. That was part of the freedom of the generation! Loose fabrics, recreational straw hats, and bright colors from bob to heels. I can remember the nights now—twinkling stars above the city, a slight breeze to reawaken you of how fresh and renewed the times were, and jazz music filling the air.

*(Jazz music begins to play, and crescendos into a loud roar by the end of **BART**'s remembrance.)*

The night I met Lily, I couldn't have ever had such good luck, I was just coming into town after repairing the roof on the house, when Eugene and I decided to go off to this speakeasy downtown. We didn't really fit into the cultured type of folk there, but Eugene knew the owner from his short-lived college days, so we stuck out being idle townspeople.

(Start blackout over antique shop and to raise the lights on a swinging party from the past; is on the opposite side of the stage of **BART**, **TOM**, *and* **LOUISA**.*)*

That didn't matter though, because when the party roared, everyone in the room got to roar with it.

(There is a party full of wild young swingers doing the Charleston and quickstep dances. The jazz is loud and booming. A **MAN** *is next to the door marking the exit, he hears a knock from* **YOUNG BART** *and* **YOUNG EUGENE** *outside.)*

MAN. Yes?

(into the slit in the door; he can just see the outsider's eyes)

YOUNG EUGENE. Jail's Ale

(the **MAN** *unlocks the door and allows* **YOUNG BART** *and* **YOUNG EUGENE** *to enter)*

Well hasn't the cat meowed tonight Bart! Look at all of these dames just waiting to be cashed!

YOUNG BART. How can you admire them? They look like blurs of colors to me.

YOUNG EUGENE. Just wait, brother, by the end of the night, you'll be seeing more than just colors.

YOUNG BART. And to think you once had a more Christian mind-set than myself.

YOUNG EUGENE. That was when we were saps, and Ma believed the war would never end and that we were to end in it. No reason to be uptight. Relax, find a Jane, and meet me back at the bar before you leave.

YOUNG BART. Whoa, leave? I didn't know you were just going to desert me when we came here.

YOUNG EUGENE. Bart, baby. This isn't a high school foot-ball game! Go and discover what lies out there, and if nothing good happens in the next thirty minutes, come find me and then I'll help you acclimate to the scene, alright?

YOUNG BART. Yeah, but what if I—

> (*EUGENE's old college friend comes from the crowd and in a fraternal manner turns* **EUGENE** *to the side.*)

FRED. Eugene! How's it going, isn't this place just as jiving as I described it to you in that letter?

YOUNG EUGENE. Fred, it's great to see you, this is my brother, Bart.

> (**FRED** *tips his straw entertainer's hat to him*)

I feel like it's been so long! How about we catch up over some gin?

FRED. Eugene, *(pulling him over to the bar)* let me introduce you to the bartender's specialty. Jack! *(calling to the bartender, who looks up accordingly)* Two of your Spice with Dice Right's tonight! So, Eugene…

> (*The two fade into conversation and cross over to the bar for their drinks, as* **YOUNG BART** *looks like a lame duck standing undecidedly at the edge of the dance floor. He eases towards the wall full of ill-postured singles, and looks around at the overly-made up women and cocky, overly dressed men.*)

YOUNG BART. All the wallflowers are wilted.

> (*A dancing, sweating flapper spins and with her partner barrel-rolling over* **YOUNG BART**, *who is disgusted by the perspiration.*)

And the bloomers don't smell like roses either.

> (*At this point, he has wandered to the area of small dining tables. He is downstage of a table with an eye-catching, elegant woman, sitting with her back to the audience alone at a candlelit table, smoking from a long stem; this is* **LILY**)

LILY. *(leaning her head directly back over the chair to comment)* That's why there's an unimaginable demand for Chanel.

> (*She retracts her head to look upstage again.*)

YOUNG BART. (*perplexedly*) Excuse me?

LILY. (*turns around completely this time to see him*) Chanel, especially number 5. It's a French perfume with rose essence in it. Deodorants are sticky and ruin the feeling of femininity that these girls already left partially behind with their locks, so they use Chanel instead.

YOUNG BART. That girl did not smell like roses. (*points to the couple that just swung past him*)

LILY. You can only use what you can afford.

(*She stands and swirls dreamlike into a very confident pose.*)

I'm Lily, by the way, Lillian Conaton.

YOUNG BART. (*quiet, nervous, and unsurely*) I'm, I'm Bart.

LILY. Well, simply Bart, how about you share a jig with me?

YOUNG BART. Well, I guess I—

(*She pulls him by the tie to the dance floor.* **YOUNG BART** *is obviously very timid during the fast dance, and* **LILY** *tries to teach him some steps. The song quickly fades into a slow dance, and* **LILY** *and* **YOUNG BART** *are standing arms-length apart.* **LILY** *bows gentlemanly and then sticks out her hand.*)

LILY. May I have this dance kind sir?

YOUNG BART. (*with sudden confidence*) My pleasure, Madame.

(*He takes her hand and they begin to dance closely. The lights start to fade as* **YOUNG EUGENE** *and* **FRED** *ease on over to the diner tables to sit with two girls. Before* **YOUNG EUGENE** *takes his seat, he looks over at* **YOUNG BART** *and smiles approvingly. The light illuminating the party becomes barely visible. The jazz music falls into a decrescendo, becoming barely audible. The light comes back up over the antique shop interior as* **LILY** *and* **YOUNG BART** *continue to dance in the shadows; the other party guests filter out occasionally representing the passage of the night.* **LILY** *and* **YOUNG BART** *are the last two dancers remaining.*)

BART. I think I realized during that dance that that was the start of the rest of my life.

(**LOUISA** *is in a dreamlike state of wonder sitting on the floor.*)

TOM. You couldn't have been that crazy about the girl so intensely, Mr. Kasich.

BART. Indeed I was, and in fact still am. Check the price tag on that dress boy and tell me how much it's worth.

TOM. *(goes and searches for a tag on the dress)* There isn't one.

BART. Exactly! I could never imagine selling one of Lillian's things, and with what she fancied, if I sold all of her possessions after she died, I wouldn't have to run an antique shop.

(**EUGENE** *enters without the others' attention.*)

TOM. Hasn't the other Mr. Kasich wanted to sell some of her things off? I mean you run the business together and if there was a way out, wouldn't he be mad at you if you denied retirement due to, well, the memory of this woman Lily?

EUGENE. *(startling* **TOM***)* Lily wasn't just a woman to Barty here. She became the wife of all wives. Also, I might not look it, but like Bart, I too am a sentimentalist. Fred and I, when we where younger, made a large sum off of our distilling business, and since we decided not to have a record of our profits because let's say, the political conflict of the time—

BART. —The National Temperance

EUGENE. Yeah, that piece of—anyways, we never invested our profits immediately into a bank, so it was never lost during the Depression. Fifteen years ago I gave the funds to split between my two sons and daughter as wedding gifts—I didn't have to, just wanted them to live out the rest of their lives with peace of economic mind. I could have easily retired with half of that sum! But then what would I do, what would I need to do? Play golf for the rest of my days? Personally, the only form of entertainment I have ever really been interested in was playing football, which who knows how many vertebrae I would break in just one scrimmage, and that ancient genre called comedy, which running this shop with ol' Bart here supplies.

LOUISA. What other things of Lily's did you keep Mr. Kasich?

BART. Pretty much everything in here that isn't made in the U.S.A. As I shared with you before, she was a classic world traveler with a French collection and photography firm, created by a man her father knew. They mainly took shots for scenic calendars and postcards, but in every country, she would pick up valuable items for me in Europe, or Egypt, India, and once China. Since I had at one point apprenticed in carpentry, she often brought back broken furniture that she found for cheap, and I would fix it up to sell at the county auction once a month. Since her passing, I did sell a lot of the things Lily brought back like the furniture, but at the same time most of her things like that dress I first saw her in are more important than any selling price to be offered.

TOM. So the dress is like that red vase, Mr. Kasich? You would never ever consider selling it?

BART. *(He walks over to the vase and picks it up caringly, looking at it as if it were a photo of* **LILY**.*)* This vase was always present in my and Lily's life together, never really the center of it, but always in the background of every memory we shared together.

(Lights start to slowly relight the young dancing couple, **BART** *walks slowly closer to the dancers' side of the stage.)*

Every time I look at this vase, I see the rose tint in her lips, the thinness of her waist, the openness of her kind, gentle soul, the sparkle of her eyes—this vase is my last untainted still frame of Lily.

(At this point, **YOUNG BART** *has twirled* **LILY** *into a final stretched out pose with her hand reaching for the*

sky. **OLD BART** *has moved over to couple holding the vase up at an angle, very near to Lily's outstretched hand. Lights over* **EUGENE**, **TOM**, *and* **LOUISA** *have dimmed, so the main focus is* **BART** *and the couple poised with a line of symmetry separating them downstage, a mirror image of what* **BART**'s *relationship was and what it has turned into. They stand completely still until the blackout ends the scene.)*

Scene 4

*(It is a jovial spring morning and **EUGENE** is teaching a giggling **LOUISA** how to dance ridiculously and dramatically to pompous, swing music playing on a record player. **TOM** is nearby setting up a game of skittles.)*

EUGENE. *(off beat and changing in tempo while swirling **LOUISA** around)* And one and two and four and one and three and five and now rotate and two and three and—

*(**EUGENE** then spins an excited **LOUISA**, who during the dance knocks over the game pieces **TOM** was arranging with her foot as she swept it ballerina-like into the air. **LOUISA** hasn't realized the fumble in her fun. **TOM** initially looks infuriated and stands, but he silently calms himself back to his seat to reset the skittles pieces. She then swirls dangerously towards the valuables on the desk, which includes the vase. **EUGENE** immediately swings her away from the valuables.)*

EUGENE. Whoa there! Let's slow down a bit. Stand on my feet, Louisa.

LOUISA. Wouldn't that hurt though?

EUGENE. Oh no! These leather shoes are so thick, you could be wearing heels and I wouldn't feel a thing!

(She stands on his feet, and now their dance is not as raucous, very similar in style to a fast, father-daughter style of dance. The record begins to skip.)

Alas, technology once again fails to mirror live performances. *(goes to the player)* Here's the problem.

(He takes a white rag and wipes the record; it becomes gray from dust.)

That's funny—I thought I cleaned this before I put it in.

LOUISA. Let me see if I can help. *(goes to player also)* Hmm, Mr. Kasich, look into the player, it's so dirty inside, I can't tell if the needle is dull or just covered in yuck.

EUGENE. I knew we should have just listened to the radio.

LOUISA. What do you mean? We can just clean it off—then it will be fine to play again.

EUGENE. If you want to clean it, I would not condemn you.

LOUISA. I don't mind. Mamma makes me dust all of her nick-knacks at home. Can you hand me that rag?

(He gives it to her and she starts to clean, standing on her tip-toes in order to reach into the player.)

TOM. Louisa, I have the board all set up.

LOUISA. Just give me a moment, Tommy.

(She thrashes the rag hastily before she finishes, in the process accumulating dust into the air. She crosses to **TOM** *and the set game of skittles as he begins to speak.)*

TOM. Do you remember how to play? It's similar to bowling, where you try to in the least amount of tries to knock down all of the…NO!

LOUISA. Ah-ah-choo!

(She sneezes loudly from the dust in the air, stumbling and knocking over all of the game pieces for a second time.)

I, umm, win?

TOM. Louisa! Why do you always have to be so accident prone! Just sit still for once. Do you ever simply focus? All I ever hear from you is either excessive giggling or uncontrollable wailing.

*(***LOUISA*** is tearing up, gradually increasing to a heavy cry.)*

Oh no. See, even though I've seen you get upset at least once for every time I think something will smoothly go as planned, I still don't know how to make you stop!

(Enter **BART***).*

BART. *(slightly out of breath and crossing to* **EUGENE***)* What's going on? I sensed unhappy child syndrome from upstairs.

EUGENE. Well, we sure do have two cases of it, although I cannot yet tell which case is more extreme. Exhibit A *(gesturing to* LOUISA*)* is soundly not in harmony while Exhibit B *(points to* TOM*)* has blown out his voice.

BART. Yes, yes. Both have similar complexions of heated faces, *(starts to stroke his chin)* although, for the presence of tears on Exhibit A I would recommend a tall glass of apple juice as a cure.

(By this point, TOM *has become extremely tense and red in the face, and looks as if he could not utter another word out of frustration.)*

EUGENE. Oh definitely, yes...

(going behind and to the side of LOUISA *to examine her reddened face; she has calmed down much but is still teary eyed.)*

...and her eyes are so tightly being closed up, the juice's vitamin C will make her be able to visualize something besides the inside of her eyelids!

BART. A humidifier would do her well, too.

EUGENE. There'd be no need for that, there is already enough steam coming out of Exhibit B's head! The girl will be alright, but now the boy, what shall we prescribe for him?

BART. Very difficult...a terrible heated complexion, I think the only cure for this one is a...a...a...

EUGENE. Yes, doctor?

BART. A lemon-flavored ice lolly!

(A small giggle comes from LOUISA*.)*

EUGENE. What! But it's so cold! I don't know if we could make him endure it!

TOM. *(annoyed)* Alright, I get it already.

EUGENE. He speaks! Quick! Doctor, go fetch that lemon flavored ice lolly before he starts seeing delusions!

BART. Come, Nurse! We need assistance in the pharmaceuticals. Stat!

EUGENE. We're on it!

> (**LOUISA,** *now returned to her jovial state, exits hurriedly with* **EUGENE.**)

TOM. Aren't you so innovative?

BART. And aren't you so cheery.

> (**TOM** *giving him a disapproving glance.*)

Don't let her affect you, kid. She means no harm—she's just unaware at her age of her effects on other people.

TOM. I can understand that, except why does she have to continuously be so bothersome! I was never that obnoxious, no matter how young I was.

BART. That's because you have a calmer personality—it's normally a good thing.

TOM. So if being a calm person is a good trait, then being a wild person must be a bad trait correct?

BART. That's not what I mean. You see, being either wild or calm are characteristics that you and Louisa differ in; you're different from each other, that's why you two clash and conflict.

TOM. So either me or Louisa has to change how we act in order to not fight anymore?

BART. Not exactly…this is difficult. Umm, maybe an analogy would help. Let's say you and Louisa are pieces in a jigsaw puzzle, and you two pieces are trying to fit next to each other, but you two pieces won't fit. You know you are supposed to fit next to each other, yet you can't figure out how. Frustration builds and you two just give up on finding a place to fit because you were confident that that was where the two pieces were supposed to join. But then, if you try pivoting your piece…

> (*uses a hand motion showing the rotation of a puzzle piece*)

…you'll see that Louisa's piece will fit into another one of your sides, and then you form a beautiful picture through the puzzle!

TOM. Did you take your pills this morning, Mr. Kasich?

BART. That's not the problem now. Don't you understand? If you start to look at Louisa with a different perspective than just "this annoying little sister of mine," you'll get along, or fit, and be happy.

TOM. So, then was I or Louisa wrong in our argument?

BART. No, no, no! You're missing the point, Tom! What I'm trying to get across to you is that most of your conflicts with Louisa aren't because of someone's wrong doing, but are due to the situation or perspective you two are stuck in. If you can start looking at Louisa as someone who is simply playful and will mature eventually, not now, but eventually, your anger will be less extreme.

TOM. So I have to change how I act! It's always me who has to change! I don't care anymore if I'm the big brother or not!—

BART. But Tom, you are her big brother, and when you alter your ways, Louisa will follow in your actions—like a chain reaction. Just give it a try and some time, and you two will eventually weave yourself into place.

TOM. Tolerance can only go so far, Mr. Kasich.

BART. It will go miles more than you think. Tom, I bet if I left you and Louisa in the shop alone for fifteen minutes with you really trying to be more understanding of your sister, that when I would return nothing detrimental would happen.

TOM. Is this a real bet, or are you attempting to make another analogy?

BART. This is a true bet. How about if I win, you have to dust the entire shop by tonight?

TOM. And if I win?

BART. Take your pick.

TOM. Louisa can't come in the store while I'm working for at least a week.

BART. Well then the deal is done.

(He begins to walk to behind the desk, puts on his glasses and piles the loose receipts.)

TOM. Wait! Aren't we going to shake on it?

BART. *(not looking up at him)* I can only do that if I can ask you a question first, Tom.

TOM. Ask away.

BART. *(becomes still and looks at **TOM** over his glasses)* Do you consider yourself a man?

TOM. *(shocked)* What, sir?

BART. *(calmly)* Do you consider yourself a man and responsible, being able to react humbly whether you win or loos at this bet?

TOM. Why, yes sir, I do.

BART. *(now very jolly and shuffling to **TOM**)* Then my boy, I mean, Thomas *(sticking out his hand)*.

TOM. *(enthused and shaking **BART**'s hand)* The deal is done!

BART. Yes sir!

(They stop shaking and there is a pause.)

Oy! Eugene!

EUGENE. *(returning with **LOUISA** eating a popsicle and holding another)* Yes, Captain! What ere your problem be?

BART. A voyage is to be made! Me anchor has rusted to the bottom of Davy' Jones' Locker, and I need to send in for a new one! *(grabs an envelope from the desk and holds it up)*

EUGENE. Argh, how long will it be for us to be back before the storm waves in?

BART. I'd say about fifteen minutes and a bottle of rum.

TOM. Fifteen—no, not now Mister!—

BART. And there's no need for any extra sailor's for this voyage, but we do need two scallywags to shine up the treasures of lost souls. *(pointing to a box labeled "broken products")*

EUGENE. Now which two Mateys can we find to take on the job, eh?

LOUISA. *(saluting)* Ay! Ay! Me Captain!

BART. Ok, we'll be back soon, and remember sailor, Tom—

TOM. Don't lower down more than thirty percent, yeah, I know.

EUGENE. Good work, mates; be back before the tide!

(**BART** *and* **EUGENE** *exit,* **TOM** *looking bothered and* **LOUISA** *innocently with her popsicle.*)

TOM. Okay, Louisa, guess what you're going to help me do.

LOUISA. Yes, Tom?

TOM. *(walking over to and picking up the "broken products" box)* You and I are going to fix all of these gray little treasures.

LOUISA. *(excitedly)* I can help! Which one do I get to fix?

TOM. Whichever one you want as long as you try to keep quiet.

LOUISA. Can I fix the clock?

TOM. But that's one of the hardest items to fix—I mean sure, Louisa, you can work on it.

LOUISA. Oh goody! And Tom.

TOM. Yes?

LOUISA. Here's your ice lolly.

(*She hands it to him, and he takes it warmly.*)

(**TOM** *starts to work on the chair from before, setting aside the popsicle on the counter, not noticing* **LOUISA** *with a marker drawing a face with large, cartoon features on the clock's front.*)

TOM. How is your fixing coming along?

LOUISA. Swell! I'm already done.

TOM. Already done? *(He turns around and becomes exasperated)* Louisa! What did you do to it?

LOUISA. I gave the clock a new face—it's a happy one too. See, I got its smile to stretch from the nine to the three!

TOM. *(keeping his temper down)* It's-it's-it's great. Can you put in on the sales desk for me to clean off—I mean polish later?

LOUISA. No problem, brother.

> *(As she sets the clock on the desk, the door chimes bring the pair's attention to a pesky, self-important* **WOMAN** *in a red evening dress who sways unnecessarily through her stride. She is accompanied by her 5 year-old* **SON**, *who is silently pouting.)*

WOMAN. *(To* **CHILD**) Daddy said we could find an old candelabra in this shop, Sweetums. Until then you'll just have to wait 'til we get home to eat something. Oh, hello there.

> *(seeing* **TOM**)

Do you know where a wooden, cherry-stained, decorated candelabra might be found in this shop? My husband is a family friend of the Kasich's and he said that he found a marvelous candelabra the other day. He has great taste, if you haven't already realized by talking to me. Anyways, did you find it yet?

TOM. *(quite appalled)* Umm, wait Ma'am. Let me search around for it. Cherry, you said?

WOMAN. Oh, why yes! Our entire living set is all cherry; it's the most elegant of the woods. I don't understand how people can stand for less, as if oak is still even considered an option.

> *(***TOM*** searches around for the candelabra with no luck.)*

You find it yet, boy? It would be dreadful for there to be nothing in the center of my mantle piece for yet another night. Oh, now what could this be?

> *(She comes across* **LOUISA**'*s fixed clock on the desk.)*

This, why, this is a most striking piece.

TOM. What? Ma'am, that clock is broken; you don't want to buy that—

WOMAN. Nonsense young man! Art is what glitters these days. How much for this material expression?

TOM. Umm, seven dollars.

WOMAN. *(taking a ten dollar bill out of her purse and handing it to* **TOM**, *who has moved to behind the register.)* There you are boy. Make sure to wrap it up nicely now.

(The **CHILD** *tugs on her dress)*

Hush! Hush, darling!

(She sees the popsicle.)

Young man, can I have this? *(holds up the popsicle)*

TOM. *(looks up)* Sure M'am. Here you are, your clock and three—

(She takes and unwraps the popsicle, giving it to her now happy **CHILD**.*)*

WOMAN. There you go Sweetums! Oh thank you *(takes the packaged clock)* and keep the change, singles are such wastes anyways. Bye now!

(The two exit, leaving **TOM** *in a state of disbelief. He walks over to* **LOUISA**, *scratching the back of his head in bewilderment.)*

TOM. I'd say, Louisa did you see that! Seven dollars for a broken clock with a three dollar tip? I never could have imagined it!

*(***LOUISA** *is busy and keeps her back to* **TOM**.*)*

Say, Louisa, are you mad at me? You don't seem very excited for the occasion.

LOUISA. I'm excited, just busy. Ah, and done! Look at this Tom!

(She turns around with **BART***'s precious red vase in her hands, altered to have a beautiful bouquet of fresh flowers sticking out of the cork.)*

TOM. *(with panic)* Oh my! Is that Bart's vase! We're not supposed to handle that!

LOUISA. *(very sweetly)* I know, but remember how Mr. Kasich said his favorite thing about this vase was how his wife would fill it whenever she left with fresh flowers? Considering she's gone, and this is his favorite memory of her, I thought it would make Mr. Kasich really happy. *(sees* **TOM***'s frustrated face)* But I promise you I did no harm to it, Tommy! If you look at it, I attached extra cork to the top, that way the pressure from the stems would not have any effect on the vase when in place. Oh Tommy! Please do not be mad at me!

(He walks over to the vase, takes it from **LOUISA** *and examines it. He smiles and goes to place it on the center of the desk as he talks.)*

TOM. Louisa, for you to use extra cork was a very smart idea, and you did well by not even scratching the vase. I can't believe I'm saying this, but I'm proud of you, Louisa. I didn't know you could be so thoughtful.

LOUISA. Really!?

(She crosses to the desk, residing opposite the side **TOM** *is on.)*

TOM. Really

LOUISA. Do you think that Mr. Kasich will like it?

TOM. I'm certain he will.

(blackout)

Scene 5

*(It is a rainy, dreary day in the antique shop. On another part of the stage locates **YOUNG BART**'s and **LILY**'s old bedroom from their marriage, which is made from the furniture arrangement of the shop. It is more lit in this part of the scene due to lightning.)*

*(A **YOUNG BART** is sleeping in the bed alone. It is in the middle of the night when **LILY** enters, dressed in a traveler's cloak and with her bags packed. She is crying silently as she enters, fixated on a sleeping **YOUNG BART**. She crosses to the red vase and its bouquet, stroking her fingers adoringly through its contents, and then pulls out a lily. Takes a letter out of her purse, places it on his nightstand with the flower atop it, and leaves in a downcast manner after the V.O. finishes.)*

VOICE OVER IN LILY'S VOICE. Dear Bart, I just received a wire from a colleague in Italy. He has offered me a deal I can't afford to decline. I will be in Italy on a business tour of the country for about a year. My heart aches how I couldn't prepare you for my departure, yet I am so excited for yet another exotic experience! I hope my absence will only make our marriage stronger, so that when I return, our exponential love will make up for the lost year. With love, Lily.

*(The lightning ceases and the lighting above the cashiering desk brightens revealing a grave **BART** filing though old receipts. The air is gloomy and gray, which **TOM** notices as he enters, which is signaled by the door chimes.)*

TOM. Not a very swell day outside today.

*(He takes off his rain coat and then looks up at **BART**.)*

You look quite under the weather yourself, Mr. Kasich. Anything bringing you down today?

BART. I just received some bills in the mail this morning, which are heavier than I expected.

TOM. They're not severe enough to affect the business, are they sir?

BART. The heating and lighting bills aren't too extreme when it comes to the shop, but they still create a major burden. What I can't handle is the other news I received this morning.

TOM. What might that be?

BART. My nephew, Eugene's youngest son, got in a car crash last night. He's in the hospital, and he's going to be just fine, but the job to fix him up will not be.

TOM. How badly hurt was he?

BART. Broken bones and internal bleeding—I spent all last night worrying about his injuries with Eugene, who is now too unwell to come in the shop and is trying to find a way to visit his son. Tom, go switch the "open" sign on the door to "closed." Nobody's going to come in today with this weather. Also boy, I need you to pack up every last item that we're going to bring to auction. I know I told you we needed to have it done not for a few more days, but with these circumstances, it's best to see if we could head in and try to start selling a day early.

TOM. Sure, Mr. Kasich. If we're selling at auction sooner, then doesn't that mean you'll get more income with the extra day, so you won't have to worry about your bills?

BART. *(taking off his glasses and putting down the receipts)* Tom, if we don't magically do well at auction, I'll have either two options in order to pay off my nephew Joe's medical bills—to either sell the shop, or to sell most of Lily's old things.

*(He smells the flowers that **LOUISA** stuck in the vase as he says this.)*

Selling off what is left of her would definitely give us thousands of dollars at auction, but I'm an old man, and losing these constant reminders of her would start the deterioration of her in my memory. All that's left is for us to dream for the best and what time left we have in this shop.

(blackout)

Scene 6

(**TOM** *is buying meat at the butcher's shop, which is represented by a counter down center stage with a butcher working behind it. He is carrying a list that his mother made him.*)

TOM. *(To the* **BUTCHER***)* Excuse me, but can I have a pound of sliced salami and two large chicken breasts?

BUTCHER. No problem. Are you a paper boy, son, because you're here mighty early—first customer of the day in fact.

TOM. Oh no, my mother simply needs me to run errands before I go to work.

BUTCHER. Where do you have to work this early, son?

TOM. At the antique shop down the corner. We're preparing to go to auction today so we need to pack up everything early, which means I have to be there early..

BUTCHER. Say, is ol' Barty finally selling some of that ancient glassware and glass-cabinet items that his wife left behind?

TOM. Hopefully not, Mr. Kasich loves her possessions more than I knew objects could be loved.

BUTCHER. But does he realize how much some of her things are worth, like that red vase of his that he has on his store counter? If I owned a vase like that, I wouldn't let sit anywhere it could be accidentally knocked over. When I went in there with my sister, who knows plenty about her vases—she works for the art museum in town mind—estimated that that vase is $2,700 or more with today's demand.

TOM. Did your sister tell Mr. Kasich how much she thought it was worth?

BUTCHER. Oh she tried, loves to what she calls "educating the community," but ol' Barty wouldn't listen, as if he didn't want to know its true value. Say boy, can you do me a favor and try to convince the man to put some safer measures on his shop?

TOM. What do you mean?

BUTCHER. *(leaning in towards* **TOM***)* With a shattered window or a kick to the front door with its rusty locks, anyone could break in and rob Bart and Eugene of the small fortune they still possess. Who knows, even if one of them were behind the counter, with their frail age, a damned soul wouldn't even need a gun to overpower the Kasich brothers. Convince him to buy a lockable cabinet, or at least put some of Lily's old treasures into the safe.

TOM. I never realized the shop's potential for a burglary; I will do something about it at work today. I also really appreciate your concern for them.

BUTCHER. Bart and Eugene are two merchants on this here Lane Street that anyone can relate to. Well, here's your amount due for the salami and chicken breasts...

(He hands **TOM** *a receipt, which* **TOM** *uses as a reference to pay him.)*

...and good health to you and the Kasichs.

TOM. Thank you so much, and to you the same.

(He takes his wrapped meats from the counter.)

Mister, do you think others will be able to easily value Lily's vase like you sister did?

BUTCHER. I don't know, kiddo—you can never read most of today's people—

TOM. —which makes them extremely hard to predict. Anyways, thanks for the meats again.

BUTCHER. Anytime, anytime son.

(blackout)

Scene 7

(**TOM** *rushes into the shop. It is early morning still and the weather is gloomy. There are boxes everywhere signaling* **BART***'s eventual departure to the auction.* **TOM** *is panicked by the thought of someone easily robbing the shop while* **BART** *is gone. He rushes in looking for anything that may be valuable that is not already packed.*)

TOM. Oh no! I didn't think we were this ready for auction! *(starts to look around)* Now, what of Lily's did Mr. Kasich not pack that I can hide and keep safe?

(*He sees at first the vase, takes it and stands on a stool in order to try to hide it into an overhead cabinet.*)

It won't fit with all these flowers in it!

(*He starts to pull the flowers out as* **LOUISA** *enters, carrying a bag of bagels.*)

LOUISA. Tom! What are you doing! Those are Lily's flowers!

(*She drops the bagels on the floor.*)

TOM. Leave me alone, Louisa. I don't have too much time until we leave for auction!

LOUISA. Leave those flowers in there! They're still fresh and they make Mr. Kasich happy! Why do you want to upset him?

(*By now she has ran over to* **TOM***, trying to grab the vase from his grasp.*)

TOM. Stop that, Louisa! I'm trying to lock up the vase so it's kept safe while no one's here working the shop!

LOUISA. You're lying! You are mad that I finally made someone happy to the point where you couldn't deny it—and now you're trying to get back at me!

(*The tug-o-war over the vase intensifies.*)

TOM. Shut up Louisa! That's not it; you always think that everything is about you!

LOUISA. That's not true!

TOM. Everything you do and say supports it!

LOUISA. I hate you!

(**LOUISA** *releases her grasp on the vase, making* **TOM** *fumble backwards, losing his grip. The vase falls with a loud shatter all over the floor.*)

(**TOM** *and* **LOUISA** *are silent due to what has happened. Then,* **LOUISA** *begins to wail loudly, while* **TOM** *is completely frozen in horror.* **BART** *enters, not noticing the spread of flower petals and broken glass on the floor—all he sees is* **LOUISA** *in distress. He goes to her with the care as if she were his own child.*)

BART. What's wrong, Louisa? Don't cry you little flower, or your petals will wilt. Calm, down. I'm sure whatever happened isn't much, or it can at least be reversed.

(*At this* **LOUISA** *becomes so upset, that she stops crying and bites her lip through her silent tears. She slowly shakes her head at* **BART**, *who rises to look at* **TOM**, *whose face is shiny due to a flow of silent tears.*)

Tom, what happened?

(*At this,* **TOM** *steps backwards in shame, stepping on a piece of broken glass.* **BART** *hears the noise it makes, and looks down at the shattered contents on the floor, then at the desk,* **LOUISA**, *and then* **TOM**. **BART** *starts walking toward the biggest pile of broken glass.*)

I never thought this could happen. I kept that vase on the store desk for years, and it never got bumped or fell or even scratched. I think it was the one object in this building that forever kept its shine. Maybe I've pretended for too long, that it was invincible to harm, or to cause harm such as the tears on your little faces, and now mine.

TOM. Do you think there is any chance of repairing it? Gluing the pieces all back together would sure take a while, but it might be worth it, and maybe if we fit everything carefully together, most of its old beauty could be restored?

BART. I'm not upset about how the vase lost its beauty—I have other sources of beauty and charm that can reform an image of Lily, although I can't deny how much this sight pains me. Recall when I told you how Lily had a cork stuck in the vase before she died, and I refused to retrieve it out? This wasn't to prevent breaking a beautiful object, but to leave the memories that Lily and I created with that vase, morning breakfasts when she was home and a sweet smell of flowers when she was gone, to leave those memories untainted, finding out why the cork was placed would ruin such images of love. And now...

(He picks up the cork.)

I don't know if I can withstand my curiosity of why Lily corked the vase all of those years ago.

(He picks a small scroll of tied paper from the rubbish of glass.)

Tom, can you read this to me; I don't, I don't think I have the strength to read it first hand.

(He hands **TOM** *the scroll, who hesitantly takes it.* **TOM** *steps away from* **LOUISA** *and* **BART** *as he silently reads through the letter.)*

VOICE OVER IN LILY'S VOICE. *(somberly and forlorn)* Dear Bart, I love you too much to hurt you in person, and to see you in an unsound state before my passing would be so heart-breaking, that for my last moments on Earth, I would only see the wickedness of my human nature. This is a letter of confession, of my wrong doings to you. I see everyday how much you love me, and I know your love is blind of all my faults. Everyday I withhold forbidden truths to you, in order to maintain your happiness. This is not easy to say, but I betrayed you on my business trips, repeatedly. What is more terrible is that my business partner was whom it was with. The year I abruptly left you without notice in the middle of the night was the day I found out I was pregnant, and I wasn't strong enough to admit it to you. But now, through this letter, I can finally reveal to you the contents of my life that I was too cowardly to reveal in person. While on my other travels, I sinfully—

(The V.O. stops abruptly as **TOM** *stops reading)*

BART. What does it say, Tom?

TOM. *(turns around and looks to* **BART**, *trying to mask his solemn expression and freshly tear-stained face)* Lily wanted you to know that she loves you more than she can possibly explain. She realized how much you loved her, and forever will. She wants you to enjoy life, and learn how to let go of her in order to stop the recurring feeling of her loss. She wishes you to enjoy life with using the memories you created together as tools to find new ways to make life interesting and meaningful, not to seclude yourself in the limited enjoyment you experienced with her while she wasalive. That is Lily's last message to you.

BART. *(waits in his silent thoughts before speaking)* I don't know what to do. Does this mean I disappointed Lily for keeping all of her old things? She was a major part of my life—I don't believe I can accept her death making her not apart of my life any longer.

TOM. Lily wanted you to remember her, not to recreate her.

LOUISA. Mr. Kasich, all you need to remember about Lily, is that you loved each other.

TOM. Exactly, which makes the details of every time you expressed love for each other unimportant.

BART. So what should I do? What would Lily have wanted me to do?

TOM. I think Lily would have wanted you to sell what of hers she left behind—get rid of the material details in your life that remind you daily of her passing. Use that money to pay for your nephew's hospital bills and to fix up your shop—buy new shelves, have the floor professionally redone, invest more in your antiques; make everyday you spend in this shop with Eugene more enjoyable.

BART. It will be too hard to let her go.

TOM. It was what she wanted.

> (**LOUISA** *picks up an empty box, a dust pan, and a broom, and crosses over to* **BART**. *She gives the dustpan to* **BART** *and she sweeps in glass onto it, which he empties into the box.* **TOM** *pulls out a handkerchief and wraps his hand in it so to not cut his hand while collecting larger pieces of the vase. He buries* **LILY**'s *letter into the box during the cleaning up of shattered glass.)*

BART. Tom, go find more empty boxes.

TOM. There's not that much glass, this box alone will do—

BART. You misunderstood me, Tom. Go find more boxes— we still have some last minute items to pack. I think today is going to be a really fine day at auction.

> (*The lights transition to being a red, rosy tint.* **TOM** *runs off looking for more boxes.* **BART** *tapes up the box, which* **LOUISA** *takes and disposes of offstage. He picks up a lily from the bouquet dispersed on the floor, smells it and admires its beauty, crossing to down center stage. He smiles slightly as he smells it, entering a state of grace, yet at the same time is teary-eyed.* **BART** *maintains this expression as the lights fade to black.)*

(*curtain*)

TO WHOM IT MAY CONCERN

73

by Naomi Rawitz

CHARACTERS

CHARLIE - 16 years-old

SARA - Charlie's ex girlfriend

GARY - Charlie's best friend

MOTHER - Charlie's mom

LEXIE - Charlie's eight year-old sister

FABIOLA - Hispanic telephone operator

MACHINE - (Any of above actors except Charlie)

WOMAN - (Any of above actors except Charlie)

SETTING

The entire play takes place in Charlie's room. When the phone calls some in from Sara, Gary, Woman, and Fabiola, a spotlight comes up on one side of the stage where the actor/actress stands with a phone. Machine does not appear on stage but is an offstage voiceover. The time is present.

AUTHOR'S NOTES

The set does not have to be elaborate, A simple bed, desk and small back wall to support the jump rope are all that is necessary. Although this is a dark comedy, the characters need to be rooted in truth in order for the humor to come through in an honest way. The actress playing Fabiola does not need to speak fluent Spanish, but should be able to pronounce the Spanish words correctly. It is important that the actress playing Fabiola translates the Spanish into English in order to understand the meaning behind her words.

ABOUT THE PLAYWRIGHT

Naomi Rawitz is currently 18 years old and a senior at Adlai Stevenson High School in Lincolnshire, Illinois. She has written six short plays including *To Whom It May Concern*. She was also a playwright for three 24-Hour-Theater Projects. Naomi was a semi-finalist for two consecutive years in the Blank Theater Company's Young Playwrights Competition & Festival in Los Angeles. She also enjoys student-directing, writing poetry, and has a passion for photography. Naomi resides in Buffalo Grove, Illinois with her parents, two brothers, and sister. *To Whom It May Concern* is Naomi's first publication and she hopes it is not her last!

For Mom, who believed that I could.

(Lights up. **CHARLIE** *walks on with a pile of mail. He arrives at his desk and puts the stack of mail down. He begins to sift through the stack of mail he has just brought in.)*

CHARLIE. Bills, bills, bills, bills, adds, bills, bills, report card.

*(***CHARLIE*** stops sifting, and picks up "report card.")*

Charlie Henderson—Math-D, French-C, Biology-B plus... *(pauses)...*Thank you. *(continuing to read the grades)* English-C, History-D minus.

Teacher Comments? "See me as soon as possible, needs help, needs help, needs to grow a brain, needs help."

*(***CHARLIE*** pauses, contemplating. He throws away the report card and hits the message machine.)*

ANSWERING MACHINE. You have four new messages—that's more than usual. First message—

(beep)

(Lights up on **SARA.** *She holds the phone nervously and starts to speak.)*

SARA. *(nervous, a little paranoid)* Hey Charlie! What's up? How are you? I'm good thanks. Um…Okay. I called today, (although I REALLY hate doing this to people over the phone), to let you know that, (and don't take this personally or anything), that, you know, you and me should, like take a break for a little bit. I mean, I don't know. I don't know if we're really going anywhere. It feels like we've been standing in the same place forever, and to be honest, I really don't think it's a good use of time. And as long as I'm being honest here, you really need a better haircut. Also, it wouldn't hurt if you cut your fingernails now and then. Besides the quick fixes and everything, you should probably start to get a personality. It's hard to eat dinner with a rock. Not to be harsh or anything. It's just, well, you know…Okay, well I hope you get this message and if you want to talk or something, well it'd probably be really awkward, but like, you can Facebook me or something. Oh. And by the way, I've taken the liberty of changing our relationship status…Okay, well, bye!

(**CHARLIE** *sits down at his desk and rubs his head.*)

MACHINE. Second message—This one's a fun one.

(beep)

(lights up on **GARY***)*

GARY. CHARLAYYY! It's Gary! You won't believe where I'm calling you from!! DUDE. I've been at the Chess Team rewards gala, for making it to State, (and once again, real sorry that you didn't make it that far), and there was like this giant raffle. And you really won't believe this…

CHARLIE. *(muttering to himself)* You won?

GARY. I WON MAN!! Twenty thousand dollars!!! I KNOW RIGHT? Oh man, Charlie. If you were here, you'd be eligible for like all the other first place prizes, but yeah, I mean, maybe chess isn't really for you. Anyways, just wanted to share in the excitement! I'll see you later then—you know, you should really try out for the chess team next year. You just need to work on your strategy. Man, gotta admit, when you said, "Check-mate" after you moved your knight, dude, that was hilarious. *(yelling in background)* Alright, well I'm going to go celebrate! Peace!

MACHINE. Third message.

(beep)

WOMAN. Hello, Charlie? This is Sylvan Tutoring Center. Each year teachers from the local schools select students they want to help. If you feel stress or need help with your grades, give us a call…because your teachers already have.

MACHINE. There's at least one person on Earth that's looking out for you. That's a plus. Fourth message.

(beep)

(lights up on **SARA***)*

SARA. Hey…it's Sara again. Sorry to be such a pain but I think you still have my copy of *Superbad.* And I kinda want it back. So if you could like drop it off sometime, or I mean, just leave it in my mailbox. I'd just like it back soon, as in, as soon as possible, as in, tonight? So I guess I'll talk to you later then? Bye.

MACHINE. No more messages, thank God. Have a nice day!

*(***CHARLIE*** walks over to the fishbowl on his desk.)*

CHARLIE. Hey, Finny! How's it goin' buddy? I'm not too well, unfortunately. You're my only friend now, man. Only friend that isn't incredibly smart and rich that is. No offense or anything. You're all I got. We have to face this together. *(looks closer at the tank)* I just don't get it! How could so many things go wrong at once… are you even listening to me?? *(thinks, then taps on glass)* Finny? Hello? Finny?? *(realizes Finny is dead)* Finny?*(in agony)* Noooooooooooooooo….

*(***CHARLIE*** stands up, regaining his composure, and retrieves a box from under his bed; he unloads the box revealing a bottle of vitamin gummies, a letter, a plastic knife, a Nerf gun, duct tape, a rock, and a jump rope. He pulls out a piece of paper, and begins to review his letter.)*

CHARLIE. TO WHOM IT MAY CONCERN: In these brief 16 years I've spent on Earth, I've learned quite a bit. I've learned that waiting in four-hour lines is really not worth it because by the time you actually buy the video game system, there's a better one out. I've learned that giving is really not more rewarding than receiving because usually when I give someone a cold or bad advice, the recipient does not seem too happy. I've learned that even the best listeners can't take listening to my depressing life *(looks over at Finny)*. I've learned that when a girlfriend dumps you for not moving and your teachers call Sylvan you're pretty much the slowest person on Earth. I don't think I have the patience to move that much slower for another 80 years, so I'm making the bold choice to actually do something now. This is the last you will ever hear of me, as my time is up. I hope you know that none of this was any of your fault. I'm doing this because I have to.

(**CHARLIE** *stares at the contents of his box and ponders for a moment.*)

CHARLIE. *(Reading the gummy vitamin bottle)* DO NOT consume more than two a day.

(**CHARLIE** *stuffs his mouth with gummies. He then picks up the jump rope and duct tape. He starts to look for a spot on the wall to hang it.*)

Perfect.

(*He ties a loop out of the jump rope and with a piece of duct tape, sticks it to the wall. He examines it, and then smiles triumphantly. He slips his head under the loop and tries tightening it a little more, trying to find the perfect fit.*)

(*A voice is heard downstairs.*)

MOTHER. CHARLIE??? ARE YOU HOME???

CHARLIE. Crap.

MOTHER. CHARLIE??

CHARLIE. *(ducking under from the makeshift noose)* Hello?

MOTHER. *(knocks and opens without answer)* SURPRISE!!! We're home early!

CHARLIE. *(nervously)* Yeah, this is a surprise. *(moves over to block **MOTHER**'s view of the noose)*

MOTHER. Well you see, after Lexie and I finished the movie, we realized that there's nothing here to eat, so we decided to pick you up to go out for dinner! Lexie really wanted you to come, so we got home early, just for you!

CHARLIE. Thanks Mom. How was the movie?

MOTHER. It was interesting, sort of dark actually. It was this animated film about a caterpillar with funny glasses. Imagine that! The whole time, all he does is watch all his friends bloom into these beautiful butterflies, but he remains the same. And he hits all these crisises like excessive weight-gain from the vegetation he's been feeding on, and losing all of his friends as they fly off to the rest of their lives. And at the end, he realizes that he never really was a caterpillar, but a centipede, and that he basically would live the rest of his life in the dirt. Oh, and the funniest part? His name was Charlie! I don't think that Lexie grasped the whole concept, but it was a good story. It's a good thing I did come home early though- it's a pigsty in here! What is all this?

(She starts to move towards the table where the note is.
CHARLIE *beats her to the table and crumples up the note nervously.)*

CHARLIE. Oh, this is just some stupid schoolwork. Just a rough draft, don't worry about it.

MOTHER. And why in the world is there a jump rope on the wall?

CHARLIE. *(improvising)* We have this project for science. We have to tie ourselves to a wall, and measure the resistance there is when we're trying to break from it.

MOTHER. That's great that you're doing your homework, Charlie. But isn't there any other place to do experiments other than on the newly painted walls? Those cost a lot. I want this room cleaned up now.

CHARLIE. *(rushing her out)* K, Mom, I'll start ASAP.

MOTHER. And don't forget to dust!

CHARLIE. Seriously, Mom? I've got...stuff to do.

MOTHER. Charlie—it looks like the Dust Bowl in here.

CHARLIE. What?

MOTHER. Fine. I'll do it. *(pulls a handkerchief out of her shirt and starts to dust frantically around the room)* You never know when you'll need to get some dusting done! *(sees one trophy sitting on Charlie's counter)* Honey! Look at this! I didn't know you won a trophy!

CHARLIE. *(weakly)* It's an honorable mention from the treading water competition at day camp.

MOTHER. And to think that a mother wouldn't know about such a big accomplishment!

CHARLIE. Sorry, Mom. Are you done yet?

MOTHER. *(walks towards him and smiles)* Yes, sweetheart. Now get some work done. *(leans in closer to his face as if inspecting)* Oh you've got some schmutz on your face! Let me get that. *(rubs his face with her finger)*

CHARLIE. Mom. I can clean my own face.

MOTHER. I'm your mother, it's my job. Hurry up and finish that homework please.

*(**MOTHER** exits. **CHARLIE** watches her leave and unfolds paper and continues to write.)*

CHARLIE. TO WHOM IT MAY CONCERN: When I'm gone, do not feel the need to dust my room. The particles rise into the air–and fall seconds later. There is absolutely no point. And why does paint cost so much if something as simple as duct tape will ruin it? Duct tape is supposed to be the cure for everything and anything. And honestly–how clean can you make your room? I could spend another four years cleaning, and it still wouldn't be good enough. Once I'm gone it'll just stay frozen this way, until at least someone has the courage clean up a "pigsty." I highly respect the man or woman who does.

*(**CHARLIE** gets up from the desk and starts stuffing his face with more vitamin gummies. Before he can finish, **MOTHER** calls.)*

MOTHER. Charlie??

CHARLIE. *(mouth full)* Uh yeah?

MOTHER. Are you ready for dinner yet?

CHARLIE. *(struggling to swallow all of it)* Not quite.

MOTHER. Okay, well I'm thinking we'll go out for your favorite tonight. "Breakfast for dinner!"

CHARLIE. OK, Mom. Thanks.

(**CHARLIE** *quickly grabs a pen and the crumpled piece of paper. He continues from the original message and reads as he writes.*)

CHARLIE. TO WHOM IT MAY CONCERN: It has come to my attention that this family has a weird obsession with mixing around the times for meals. I don't get it. What's so special about eating fried foods covered in syrup at night instead of morning? It doesn't change anything. It's the same food. And since when has it been my favorite?

MOTHER. *(knocks on door, and once again opens without answer)* Charlie? I brought up your laundry that you forgot to put away. All of your socks were inside out so they're still wet. I don't know how many times I ask you to turn them fully one way or another. It makes the job more difficult for me and there's no benefit to having cold, wet socks.

CHARLIE. *(trying to be sincere)* Oh. Sorry about that.

MOTHER. Still working? We'd really like to leave soon. Lexie is getting hungry.

CHARLIE. Oh. Yeah. No, I forgot to copy something down. I just need to review these answers.

MOTHER. Charlie- you really shouldn't cheat. It's a terrible habit.

CHARLIE. No...What I was saying was...

MOTHER. I don't want to hear excuses, Charlie. You know that cheating is what people do when they give up on everything. There will be no cheaters in this family! Now please be ready in a couple, so we can get there before the "The Wonderful World of Waffles" gets too busy.

CHARLIE. Okay. Be down in a couple.

MOTHER. Okay, well hurry up Charlie. Think about all those waffles just waiting for you on the griddle!

(**MOTHER** *leaves.* **CHARLIE** *flattens out the note once again.*)

CHARLIE. TO WHOM IT MAY CONCERN: I'm sorry you think I'm a cheater. Another thing—wet, cold, socks may not be so bad for people that don't have any socks at all. Did you ever think about that? Also, I wouldn't mind wearing wet, cold socks on a hot day. Think about the favor you could be doing your feet. And I really hate waffles. They're basically just soggy pancakes with more empty space. And pancakes aren't even that good either. I hope that in the future they come up with something to eat for dinner, or break-fast, or whenever, that is at least a little bit more exciting than a waffle. I also hope that hell does not turn out to be "The Wonderful World of Waffles." I'll find out soon enough.

(*Looks around carefully and picks up the rock and plastic knife. He starts to "sharpen" the plastic knife by scratching it rapidly against the rock.* **LEXIE** *enters Charlie's room, unannounced.*)

LEXIE. CHARLIE!!

CHARLIE. *(extremely annoyed and startled)* You think you could knock?

LEXIE. Sorry, Charlie! Are you excited for dinner?? We picked it special!

CHARLIE. Yes Lexie, but now is really not the time.

LEXIE. I'm sooooo excited! I think I'm gonna get the chocolate chip waffles- or maybe the blueberry ones, probably the chocolate, and they have the kind with ice cream but Mommy doesn't like it when I get that for dinner. I guess I'll go for the...hm...what are you going to get, Charlie??

CHARLIE. *(still sharpening the plastic knife)* I really don't care about it.

LEXIE. CMON!! It's your FAVORITE. What are you gonna get? Huh? What are you gonna get? Something chocolaty? Or blueberry-ry-ry? Or ice-creamy? Or strawberry-ry? Or meaty? Or hot? Or cold? Or…

CHARLIE. LEXIE. You are so annoying. Leave. Now.

LEXIE. But you didn't tell me what you were gonna get!!

CHARLIE. I don't care!

LEXIE. *(sees the "noose")* Ooh! You've got a jump rope! That's so cool! Can I have it? Please??

CHARLIE. No, Lexie. Can you please leave now?

LEXIE. *(walks to the door and then turns around slowly)* Charlie? I really wanted to talk to you about something, it's important and I really need your help with something.

CHARLIE. Can't you see I'm busy?

LEXIE. *(She moves over to take the jump rope from the wall and looks at it.)* It would only take a second…

CHARLIE. Not now.

LEXIE. Please??

CHARLIE. That's it! LEAVE NOW.

*(**LEXIE** stomps out, and slams the door. **CHARLIE** looks up, frustrated. The phone rings.)*

CHARLIE. Damn it.

*(Puts rock and knife down and answers phone. Lights up on **GARY**.)*

CHARLIE. Hello?

GARY. HEY MAN! I knew you'd answer!

CHARLIE. Who is this?

GARY. DUDE. You KNOW who this is.

CHARLIE. My conscience?

GARY. NO, your best friend who just won twenty thousand freaking dollars!!

CHARLIE. Oh.

GARY. Where's the excitement man? It's partayyyy time!

CHARLIE. Woo.

GARY. DUDE. Can you even hear me? It's like a major party over here. Where are you?

CHARLIE. What are you talking about?

GARY. Aren't you supposed to be here?

CHARLIE. Where are you?

GARY. Sara's Sweet Sixteen! Dude. That's pretty bad, she's your girlfriend.

CHARLIE. Was.

GARY. Aww man, she dumped you? That sucks! So Sara's single…single Sara…*(to himself)* ALRIGHT! So are you coming over…hold on. *(turns back off stage and is talking to someone at the party)* We're watching *Superbad*?! ALRIGHT. Oh. Well, I'm sure it'll turn up somewhere- Hey dude. Sorry about that, some kid stole Sara's copy of *Superbad*. What a loser, right?

CHARLIE. I have to go.

GARY. Alright, I'll see you in a couple then!

CHARLIE. Not reall–

*(**GARY** hangs up)*

*(**CHARLIE** puts the phone down, thinks, then picks up a note card from his desk. As he is about to dial, the phone rings again.)*

CHARLIE. Hello?

GARY. Yeah I'm calling to order five large pizzas. All right so the first two need pepperoni and the next two need just straight cheese. The last one…

*(pauses as **SARA** approaches)*

SARA. Make this one for me, Muscleman.

GARY. Alright. *(He smiles.)* What can I get you, Miss B-day Babe?

*(Before she can answer, **CHARLIE** realizes who has just called and speaks.)*

CHARLIE. Hello?

GARY. Wait! Is this Uncle Lou's?

CHARLIE. This is Charlie.

GARY. Oh! Sorry man! Wrong number! Ha…well, can you still get us those pizzas? *(pauses for laughter, but there is no response)* Ha ha. Alrighty then…

(**GARY** *hangs up.* **CHARLIE** *takes a big breath and then picks up a note card from his desk once again. He reads it and dials a number. He waits until the receiver picks up. Lights up on* **FABIOLA**.)

FABIOLA. Hola! Me llamo Fabiola.Te puedo ayudar?

CHARLIE. Um, is this the suicide hotline?

FABIOLA. ¿Que?

CHARLIE. Uhh inglés?

FABIOLA. No entiendo. ¿Qué es tu problema?

CHARLIE. Great. Of course I chose French over Spanish.

FABIOLA. ¿Hola, Hola? ¿Estás allí?

CHARLIE. Okay, let's start here. My name is Charlie and I am planning on killing myself.

FABIOLA. *(confused)* Me llamo FA-BI-O-LA

CHARLIE. So I SHOULD kill myself?

FABIOLA. *(surprised)* ¿Qué estoy llevando?

CHARLIE. Okay?

FABIOLA. *(flirty)* Oooh. Soló una camisa. Es rosada.

CHARLIE. What??

FABIOLA. *(overly dramatic)* ¡Oh! ¡Eres sucio! Pero soy una mujer inteligente y bonita. No estoy tan fácil cómo te gusta. ¡Mi vida es loca y no tengo tiempo para tus juegos! Necesitas ser un hombre fuerte para mí. Y si quieres ser mi novio, necesitas ser guapo. Me gusta fiestas y bailes, pero no me gusta el cine. Es aburrido y mis novios quieren mirar películas malas. ¡Y a veces, los novios no hablan conmigo! ¡Es ridículo! Estoy pensando, "¿Enserio?" ¡Soy tu novia! Lo siento. Cuándo pienso a mi novio último, me duele el corazón. ¿Puedes ayudarme? Te amo…y cuándo nos casaremos, iremos a Canadá. *(dreamy)* Sí, Canadá…hay muchos actividades para hacer. Podremos esquiar en las montañas y ver el sol todo el tiempo. Hay animales bonitos cómo venado y lobos. ¿Te gústalos? Son salvajes. Tal vez, cantaremos. Cuándo era niña, mis abuelos cantaban. ¿Puedes cantar? *(waits)* ¡Bueno! Dime más de tú. ¿Cómo eres? ¿Eres alto? ¿Eres castaño? Lo siento, pero no me gusta chicos rubios. Es sólo porque conozco a un novio pasado. Se llama Rodrigo y es rubio. ¡Él usó yo! Ugh! *(growing angry)* ¡Qué un feo, perezoso, enfermo, estúpido, gordo, sucio, lento, perro! ¡Lo siento pero si eres un rubio..adiós! *(change of heart)* ¡Pero espera! ¡Por favor, no salgas! Ummm… Oh! Tengo un chiste bueno. Okay. *(excited)* ¿Porque crucé la calle el pollo? ¡¿Tienes la respuesta?! *(pause)* No? Okay, no te preocupas, tengo un otro. Knock Knock…

CHARLIE. Who's there?

FABIOLA. Banana.

CHARLIE. Banana who?

FABIOLA. *(playful)* Knock knock.

CHARLIE. *(annoyed)* Who's there?

FABIOLA. Banana.

CHARLIE. Banana who?

FABIOLA. *(more excited)* Knock knock!

CHARLIE. *(aggravated)* Who's there?!

FABIOLA. ¡Banana!

CHARLIE. WHO?

FABIOLA. *(ecstatic)* ¡KNOCK KNOCK!

CHARLIE. I'm definitely not answering the door anymore.

FABIOLA. ¡¡¡NARANJA!!!!

(CHARLIE hangs up. FABIOLA remains on stage, uninformed that CHARLIE hung up.)

FABIOLA. ¿Estás alegre de que no dijé banana?! *(laughs, then a pause)* ¿Estás allí? ¿Hola? ¿¡Hola!?

(lights down on FABIOLA.)

CHARLIE. *(Passionately)* TO WHOM IT MAY CONCERN: I just hung up with a beautiful Latino woman named

Fabiola. She didn't care at all about returning some stupid movie. Mark this day as the first and last time a girl cared more about me than herself...not that we could understand each other... but love is the world's universal language...sort of. And you know what else? She respected my decision. *(not in letter)* Speaking of which...

(**CHARLIE** *picks up Nerf gun and fires a practice shot at the wall.*)

CHARLIE. Nice.

(A knock is heard on the door.)

LEXIE. Charlie?

CHARLIE. Yeah?

(**LEXIE** *enters.*)

LEXIE. Mommy wanted me to tell you that we're leaving now.

CHARLIE. Ok.

(beat)

LEXIE. Aren't you coming?

CHARLIE. I don't know, Lexie, I've just got so much work to do.

LEXIE. But, Charlie....

CHARLIE. You can still have fun without me, the movie was fine, wasn't it?

LEXIE. But it's not so much fun when you're not there. I have no one to laugh with about Mom's stupid jokes.

CHARLIE. They're not always stupid.

(**LEXIE** *gives a knowing look.*)

CHARLIE. Okay, maybe they are. Hey, I thought you liked spending one-on-one time with Mom.

LEXIE. That's only because you're always in such a bad mood. I'd rather be with you sometimes. Especially when all Mom wants to do is the dishes.

CHARLIE. Doing the dishes is better than doing homework. Wait till you get older.

LEXIE. But if I wait till I get older, you'll already be off to college. And then there's no time left.

CHARLIE. Well, I guess you're right. I mean, time moves a lot faster than we think.

LEXIE. Especially when you're not watching the cookies you're baking and they end up burning. Mom does that all the time you know.

CHARLIE. Yeah, I know, I just wish there was a way you didn't have to wait the whole time for the cookies to bake, sometimes it feels like forever.

LEXIE. Yeah, but it helps me sometimes, when the smell of cookies starts filling the kitchen. And then I know it won't be too long before we get to eat them!

(pause)

Charlie? Can I talk to you about something?

CHARLIE. Sure Lex, what's up?

LEXIE. There's this girl Julie in my class. She's really good at math.

CHARLIE. And?

LEXIE. She laughs at me a lot because I don't get the problems right away all the time like she does. And she always stares at me while I'm trying to do the problems, cause she already finished!

CHARLIE. Are you serious? It doesn't matter who gets the problems right first.

LEXIE. I don't know. Most of the other kids get it. I feel like I'm the only one who's so slow. One time, all of the kids in my class finished and Julie told them to count how long it would take me to finish. They started calling me "Loser Lexie."

CHARLIE. That's awful! She has no right to say such a mean thing. You shouldn't have to deal with this by yourself. Have you talked to the teacher about it?

LEXIE. No…I don't think that anybody understands like you do, Charlie.

CHARLIE. Did you tell Julie how you feel?

LEXIE. It's really hard. She makes me feel like I'll never be able to get it. I wish I was smart like Julie. The worst, is when she starts yelling math problems out loud. And she says, "LEXIE WHATS TWO PLUS THREE?" and I start to answer but she says, "IT'S FIVE STUPID! YOU SHOULD GO BACK TO KINDERGARTEN, WHERE YOU BELONG."

CHARLIE. Don't ever say you wish you were like Julie. Someone who puts other people down is not a good person. Bad behavior doesn't get you anywhere. She's not the wonderful, fun, loving sister that you are, and she never will be. And I don't like the way she's treating you at all.

LEXIE. I don't know how to stop her. Maybe I am really stupid.

CHARLIE. Lexie. You're not stupid. And who cares about a couple of math problems? There are always going to be times in our lives when we want to give up, when there are problems we don't get. *(More affected)* Doesn't mean we can just say "I'm stupid" and quit. Doesn't mean that we convince ourselves we're not worth it. It's like baking cookies. You don't just give up after you burn a batch.

LEXIE. Yeah. That means we could never have cookies again!

CHARLIE. Exactly, and all because some "Julie-girl" said so. Who is she anyways?

LEXIE. Her name is Julie Sanders. She has an older sister. I think her name is Sara. Don't you know her?

CHARLIE. Yeah, I think I've talked to her once or twice. She's not much nicer than her younger sister.

LEXIE. Guess it runs in the family!

CHARLIE. *(smiling)* I guess so.

LEXIE. And we can say that amazing-ness runs in our family because you and me have each other.

CHARLIE. We are pretty amazing, aren't we?

LEXIE. Yeah, I just hope Julie doesn't laugh at me again tomorrow. Sometimes, I just want to run away and hide when she does that, because all the other kids laugh too.

CHARLIE. I'll be there for you through this, Lex, don't you worry about it. We're going to make it through this patch together.

MOTHER. *(calling from downstairs)* Are you guys ready yet?

LEXIE. *(yelling to* **MOTHER***)* YES, MOM! I just have to run to my room to get some socks! *(to* **CHARLIE***)* Mine are all wet! *(rolls eyes)* Are you coming, Charlie?

CHARLIE. Yeah, I'll be right down.

*(***LEXIE*** goes to leave.)*

CHARLIE. Wait. Lexie?

LEXIE. Yeah?

CHARLIE. Here, *(takes down the jump rope)* you can have my jump rope.

LEXIE. Really? *(He nods.)* Thanks, Charlie!

*(***LEXIE*** exits.)*

CHARLIE. TO WHOM IT MAY CONCERN: So what did I really learn in these brief 16 years? I learned that you can have all the money in the world, but you'll always be a loser on the chess team. That waffles aren't really that bad, everyone gets wet socks every once in a while, centipedes make it too, sometimes the burnt cookies taste the best, and maybe, there is such a thing as the perfect stranger.

*(***LEXIE*** enters unannounced.)*

LEXIE. Let's go, Charlie! What's taking you so long?

CHARLIE. I'll be down in a minute.

LEXIE. *(nagging)* But we want to go now.

CHARLIE. *(aggravated)* OK, Lexie. Please leave.

LEXIE. *(Crosses arms and watches* **CHARLIE** *for a moment, waiting for him to exit. She loses her patience.)* Hurry up already!

CHARLIE. *(sternly)* I said OK. I won't get ready until you leave.

(**LEXIE** *rolls her eyes and exits.* **CHARLIE** *throws the items back into the box. Suddenly the phone rings.* **CHARLIE** *answers. Lights up on* **FABIOLA**.)

CHARLIE. *(in disbelief)* Hello?

FABIOLA. ¡Hola Charlie!

CHARLIE. Hola.

(**CHARLIE** *smiles as lights fade to black.*)

OTHER TITLES AVAILABLE FROM BAKER'S PLAYS

A FATHER'S SECRET

Alexandra Dennett

Drama / 6m, 2f / Areas

**Winner of the 2007 Baker's Plays High School
Playwriting Competition**

What if your entire world is taken away from you, twice? Paige was seven when her parents died in a car accident, and ever since then one of their friends, Eddie, has taken care of her. He's a strict guardian, but she has an active life and good friends and generally enjoys a rather stable and happy existence. Then one day, eight years after Eddie took her to live with him, the police barge in and arrest him for kidnapping her. They inform her that her parents weren't dead when he took her away, and that her father is still alive. But Eddie has been her sole parent, and a good one, for the majority of her young life and Paige resists the ever-growing realization that the man she trusts most is not who she thought he was.

OTHER TITLES AVAILABLE FROM BAKER'S PLAYS

STARSTRUCK!

Laura Gary

Comedy / 6m, 13f, chorus

**1st Place Winner of the 2002
Baker's Plays High School Playwriting Contest**

The rock musical for the new millennium, is the story of a teen pop singing sensation, Daphne, who is returning to perform her hit single, "Starstruck," at her high school prom. The kids at Messina High are all excited about the upcoming event. The senior class president, Claudia, decides she wants everyone to have a date for the prom, especially her feuding friends, Ben and Bebe (loosely based on the Shakespearean characters Benedict and Beatrice in *Much Ado About Nothing*). Claudia attempts to get them together by using modern technology to spread rumors that Ben likes Bebe and Bebe likes Ben. When Ben and Bebe find out what's going on, they decide to give Claudia and her boyfriend a little bit of her own medicine, and everyone winds up unhappy. Depressed and discouraged, the kids go to their haven—the mall—to lift their moods. At the mall, the girls get ready for prom, and the two main couples resolve their differences. Happy again, all the kids go to the prom, where Daphne appears and everyone sings "Starstruck" in the surprising, funny finale.

Starstruck! has been called "*Bye Bye Birdie* meets *Grease* with songs about shopping, going online and getting a date" by the pop music critic of the *Atlanta Journal/Constitution*. It's a play today's teens crave—one written by them and for them and enjoyed by all ages.

OTHER TITLES AVAILABLE FROM BAKER'S PLAYS

DRAMATIC DEBUTS

Various Authors

High School, Community Theatre

Winners of the Baker's Plays High School Playwriting Competition

Baker's Plays has been an advocate for theater in schools for over one hundred years. In the spirit of that commitment, we offer this playwriting competition for High School students. Plays may be about any subject and of any length. It is our hope that this competition will encourage aspiring high school authors to explore the creative possibilities of writing for the stage.

The winners of the 2008 competition:

Writer's Block by Samuel French - 1st Place
Mechant Enfant by Samuel Mayer - 2nd Place
The Metronome by Gabriel Neudstadt - 3rd Place
Unwanted Adventure by Brandon Johnson - Honorable Mention

The winners of the 2009 competition:

If I Were Your Superhero by Laignee Barron - 1st Place
A Funeral For Mittens by Samuel French - 2nd Place
Making Babies by Paxton Farrar – 3rd Place

The winners of the 2010 competition:

Hesperides by Gabrielle Hoyt-Disick - 1st Place
Keeping Company by Michael Bontatibus - 2nd Place
So by Zoë Wilson - 3rd Place
Navy Blue Tiles by Katarzyna Roszczeda - Honorable Mention

CALLING ALL PLAYWRIGHTS!

DRAMATIC DEBUTS
Baker's Plays High School Playwriting Competition

Be a published playwright…
Bring us your **BEST**, **BOLDEST** and most **BRILLIANT** plays.

Please visit BakersPlays.com for more information on how to submit your play and win!

BAKERSPLAYS.COM